Manufactured in the United States of America.

Cover design and website by Blue Boy Media

ALSO BY A.R. SHAW

23: The Street History of a Shoe

The Documentary

www.23novel.com

Thanks to my family, friends and everyone who inspired me before, during and after the completion of this project.

—A.R. Shaw

TWENTY-THREE

A NOVEL

CHAPTER I

Anyone can handle addition, but it takes a strong person to survive subtraction. –Tina Hall

"Man, hit him again! He think we playin'. "

"Forget that. Take 'em. I got 'em by the neck. He ain't goin' nowhere!"

I could have died that night. In a sense, death did arrive by killing what was left of me, and giving birth to something more vicious on that cold Chicago street near Metcalfe Park.

Before my birth, my mother knew that I would have to deal with an important subtraction in my life. She once told me the story of how she met my father when she was a 17 year-old high school senior. She described him as a tall, lanky 25 year-old street ball player who peddled heroin at night and played basketball at Washington Park during the day. His name was Calvin Royals, but people on the West Side called him C-Roy. My mom talked about how she was captivated by the black 1968

Lincoln Continental he drove around Chicago.

She first caught a glimpse of the car while visiting her best friend Melinda, who stayed on South Morgan Street. She said the glossy black paint that reflected light like a mirror, and the virgin clean white wall tires gave her goose bumps. They made eye contact as he drove by at about 10 miles per hour. He looked at her while leaning back in the driver's seat with his right arm stretched out, and his right hand clutching the top of the steering wheel. He kept his eyes on her, but didn't say a word as he crept down the street. A couple of months later, they were introduced to each other at Washington Park after one of his basketball games.

Melinda and my mom went to the park to hang out and watch some of the best playground ball players that Chi-town had to offer. The pick-up games at Washington Park drew hundreds of spectators. Anyone who was anybody on Chicago's street scene was there. On that summer afternoon in 1973, my mom sat in the stands and watched as C-Roy dunked, dribbled and shot jumpers as effortlessly as he breathed.

After the game, my mom found herself staring as C-Roy wiped his face with a towel and slid a pick through his short Afro. He and another ball player approached her and Melinda. Melinda then introduced my mom to her boyfriend, Scoop. Before they could shake hands, C-Roy moved in front of Scoop and gently grabbed my mother's right wrist.

"I know you," C-Roy said, as he pulled her closer. "I don't think you do," she replied.

"Well, what can I do to change that?"

"I'm not really sure. Are you worth knowing?"

"It depends on what you consider worthy. Between me and you, we both see this city the way we see this city. I might like the way you see it. But let me invite you to get a glimpse of it from my view. Maybe you will like how I see it. If you don't like it, then no I'm not worthy."

C-Roy offered my mother a ride home and she agreed to go with him. She said that she felt like a queen riding in that black Lincoln while Bobby Womack played on C-Roy's 8-track car stereo. People on the corner of West 63rd Street waved because they admired C-Roy and the girl sitting next to him.

"What's up, young blood!" "What it be like C-Roy!" C-Roy honked his horn and put his hand out of the window to acknowledge the people who respected him. That kind of power was unfamiliar to my mother.

"You get hungry don't you?" C-Roy asked my mom as he drove.

"At times, don't we all?" my mother answered.

"Is this one of those times for you?"

"Could be."

"There's this place called The Drake. They got some of the best lobster in Chicago. I say we make it a date."

C-Roy took my mother to dinner at The Drake Hotel and afterward invited her to his apartment that night. She realized that she was in a vulnerable position, but her 17 year-old mind didn't know how to decline such an appealing offer.

Two months later, my mother discovered she was pregnant. She hid her pregnancy for an entire month afraid of what her life would become with a child. She eventually gained the strength to tell her parents. They both insisted on meeting with C-Roy. But C-Roy rarely stayed in one spot. My mom went to his place several times and made a few visits to Washington Park without seeing a trace of the guy whose baby she was carrying. She eventually contacted Melinda to reach C-Roy through

Scoop.

Three weeks later, C-Roy was pounding on her parents' door on a late November night during a steady downpour of rain. My mother unlocked the front door and a drenched C-Roy walked inside wearing a black leather jacket and a brown wool brim hat. She attempted to embrace C-Roy, but he stepped to the side and said, "Melinda told me there was an emergency." She shut the door and asked him to sit down. However, C-Roy continued to stand. When she told him about her situation, his response clarified their relationship for my mom.

"I don't have time for no baby," C-Roy said. "Matter of fact, I don't think it's mine. You're not about to trap me. You might just want to get rid of it!" C-Roy's commotion woke my mother's parents. They both walked into the living room to investigate the noise. My mother's father, Clarence, spoke up to gain control.

"You need to lower your voice in this house young man! And what's all this fussing about Tina?" Clarence asked.

"Daddy, this is Calvin, the friend that I was telling you and momma about."

"Oh, so this is the guy who wants to lay around and leave when it's time to stay around. Where are you from son?"

"I don't think you should be concerned about that pops. Just mind your business, alright," C-Roy said.

"If you're dealing with my daughter, in my house, then it is my business!" Clarence declared as he moved closer to C-Roy. My mom and her mother, Pearl, stepped in between the two men. C-Roy spit out the toothpick that was in his mouth and reached into his pocket. My mother looked down and noticed that a silver switch blade was in his right hand.

"Old man, do you know what I'll do to you?" C-Roy

asked while holding the blade near his right leg. Clarence
pulled my mother and Pearl away from C-Roy and
positioned them behind him. He then looked directly into
C-Roy's eyes and said,

"Listen boy. I spent five years in Korea fighting a war with
an enemy that would kill as easily as if they were taking a
crap— all while dealing with racist soldiers who could care
less that I was fighting with them under the same flag. And
after risking my life overseas, I come back to this country
and find that I still can't eat at certain places in the South. So
there ain't nothing that you can do to me that'll make me
break. I've seen everything but God himself. And if you're
man enough to put me closer to Him, go ahead. Do what
the hell you gotta do!"

C-Roy closed the switch blade and eyed my mother as his
nostrils flared. He told her he would do what he could to help,
but he didn't have time for a relationship. Her eyes watered.
She didn't understand how someone so perfect, could not love
her or the child that he helped to create. In a sense, I believe
that she had dreams of riding in that Lincoln again with a man
whom she and everyone in the neighborhood loved. All the
time waving at people who admired them like the president and
the first lady. She wanted to know what it felt like to wear the
last name, Royals. She would have loved to sit in the stands as
C-Roy's woman and watch him annihilate dudes on the playgrounds of Chicago. She wanted to be with him in his world,
but he would not allow it.

C-Roy put his hat on and flipped up his collar. He stepped
outside with a slow stride that was unaffected by the torrential
rain. After closing his car door, he revved the engine and the
dual pipes roared. He drove down West End Avenue. From her

front door, my mom watched the Lincoln until it made a left on Mason. It was the last time she saw that car and the man who owned it.

My born day occurred on the 14th day of May in 1974. Hours after my birth, my mother named me Minus. She said the minus symbol was the most powerful symbol in math. She believed that the subtracting of something would make an individual work and think harder to retrieve what they had lost. She would say, "Anyone can handle addition, but it takes a strong person to survive subtraction."

By the time I was six, my mother was able to add a few dollars to her bank account when she got hired as a receptionist at Mercy Hospital on the South Side. She used to say that extra baggage found its way around her hips, due to the long hours she spent sitting at the front desk. But her size didn't deter dudes who would often help her carry grocery bags when we stepped off of the CTA in route to my grandparents' home in Oak Park. Sometimes, guys would come by to take her out, but no one stayed around long enough to be remembered.

We eventually moved from my grandparents' home into an old greystone apartment off of West 26th Street. My grandfather packed all of our belongings into his station wagon and drove until we reached a three-story red brick building. He parked his station wagon and I saw the bright red steps which marked the entrance into the greystone that housed three other families. Once inside, we walked up two flights of hardwood stairs to get to the apartment that contained two bedrooms, one bathroom, a kitchen, plus a living room that provided enough space for a few guests.

My mother decorated our apartment with flowers and pictures of friends and family. She bought a tweed green sofa that did little to complement the blue wall paper and brown wool rug that she placed in the middle of the living room floor. Above the couch, she hung a gigantic picture of *The Last Supper* that was given to her by my grandmother.

My mother did all that she could to make the inside of our apartment comfortable. But outside was less than cozy. A few days after we moved in, we were both startled awake in the middle of the night by the sound of a fist pounding on our door. My mother opened the door to a half-dressed woman with scratches and bruises on her face. She let the woman inside, wrapped a towel around her and called the police. After that incident, my mother began to pay closer attention to the problems in our new neighborhood.

Trouble usually occurred when older teenagers and dudes in their early 20s would gather in front of our building for hours. It became commonplace to see them on the red steps shooting dice and drinking from brown paper bags.

By 1986, crack cocaine use was on the rise and the entire neighborhood began to change. The "porch boys," as the older residents called them, went from shooting dice to shooting at rival gangs. The "porch boys" eventually lost their hangout spot to a crew from the Dearborn projects. They could no longer hang around those steps when the Dearborn boys decided that they wanted that location to sell drugs to the junkies and hypes who walked down West 26th.

My mother wanted to shield me from what took place outside by limiting me to play near the front door in the apartment's hallway. But on Sundays, my grandfather would visit our apartment and take me to the playground at Dunbar Park. For a while, it was the only time that I could play outside in my neighborhood.

When I was seven, I remember walking over plastic bags, candy wrappers and beer cans to reach the swings and sliding board at the playground. I didn't understand the difference between rich and poor at that age, but I did notice a difference between my neighborhood and the neighborhoods I saw on TV.

My favorite show at the time was *Silver Spoons*. It was about a kid named Ricky who lived in a mansion and appeared to own every toy that was ever made. He even had a miniature train that would take him from room to room in his house. I use to dream about waking up in the house that was next door to Ricky's. The house was a six-story brick mansion with a yard the size of a football field and a swimming pool with crystal clear water. There was an arcade room with Pac-Man and Donkey Kong. Board and card games like UNO, Monopoly and Connect Four were in another room. A special room with several TV's played cartoons like the *Smurfs*, *He-Man* and *Fat Albert*. And the toy room had thousands of G.I. Joe and Transformer action figures. I knew that if I lived in Ricky's neighborhood, everything that I wanted would be in arm's reach.

As my grandfather pushed me on the playground swing, I asked him why my apartment didn't look like the home on *Silver Spoons*. He said it was just TV, but his answer didn't satisfy me.

"So no one really lives like that?" I asked.

"Yeah, they just don't live like that where you stay," he answered before letting out a hacking cough.

"So why can't people where I stay, live like Ricky and the other people on *Silver Spoons*?"

"Well, they can. But they would probably have to get a better job and move."

"Why do people have to move? Why can't this place be

as good as the place on *Silver Spoons*?"

My grandfather stopped pushing the swing and stepped a few inches away before turning around. He removed his black frame glasses, wiped the lenses with a handkerchief and placed them slowly back onto his face. He removed his blue baseball cap, exposing his gray hair, and began to speak. "Minus, you ever see anyone around here or even at your school who looks like Ricky?" I thought about his question for a couple of seconds and answered. "I've seen police, firemen and mail men who look like Ricky."

He restated the question. "Other than people in a uniform, have you ever seen anyone at your school or where you stay who looks like Ricky?" I thought again and answered. "No."

My grandfather then explained how barriers were set up to keep blacks away from whites, and the poor disconnected from the rich. He said that every state in America had traces of segregation, but Chicago was more segregated than any place in the South. The most ironic part was that Chicago was founded by a black man named Jean Baptiste Pointe DuSable in 1779. By 1818, the state of Illinois created Black Laws to discourage blacks from living in the state. He said that the legal segregation continued into the 1930s. At that time, blacks from Mississippi migrated to Chicago in large numbers. The racial tension ran high, and riots broke out between blacks and whites. Adding to the frustration was the housing situation. Since the slum areas were overcrowded, the Chicago Housing Authority was created to provide housing for the poor. While the plan was to build housing on vacant lots in middle- and upper middle-class neighborhoods, the CHA chose instead to build vertical public housing in slum areas. Chicago became known for having the most notorious projects in the world — Cabrini Green, Robert Taylor

Homes, Ida B. Wells Homes, Stateway Gardens, Trumbull Park Homes, and Dearborn Homes. Dearborn Homes consisted of 16 buildings that were six to nine stories high. From my bedroom window, I could see the high-rises standing like brick stilts in the sky.

Some considered the projects as little more than open prisons which housed thousands of poor black families in forgotten areas of the South Side and West Side of Chicago. They became isolated sections of the city where blacks rarely left, and whites never went.

During my childhood, my grandfather was my best friend. I could always count on him to make my days less boring. We would watch sports together, go on fishing trips to Braidwood Lake, and he even taught me how to fight. He realized I needed a lesson the day he picked me up from my elementary school and noticed the angry mug on my face as I walked to his green Volvo station wagon.

"What's wrong with you boy? You look madder than a road lizard," my grandfather asked as I sat in the passenger seat and slammed the door with my thin arms. "Big Lenny Green said he's gonna fight me tomorrow because he thinks I stole his pencil. But I didn't steal it!" I replied.

"Calm down son. I know you didn't steal it. You know you didn't steal it. And Big Lenny Green knows you didn't steal it either."

"Well, why is he trying to fight me if he knows I didn't steal it?"

"He's just testing you."

"Testing me? Like a spelling test?"

"Sort of like that. See life ain't nothing but a series of tests and people will be testing you in different ways until the day that you die. When you get older, most people gonna test you mentally by seeing how smart and headstrong you are. They'll challenge you with words. But the tests you get now at your age are mostly physical. Wrestling and fist-fighting is a young boy's way of figuring out his own strengths and weaknesses as it relates to those around him. Your worth will be tested and you have to be prepared for the challenge."

Later that evening, my grandfather took me to his house and taught me how to box. As a former boxer in the Army, he knew what it would take for me to protect myself. He showed me how to keep my feet apart in order to maintain the proper balance. He then opened his hands, raised them near his chest and yelled, "Jab. Jab. Right. Jab," as I hit his hands with my small fists. I even practiced in the mirror when he dropped me off at home.

The next morning, I walked into my 2nd grade classroom with the swagger of a boxer walking into the ring. But Big Lenny Green never confronted me about his pencil and I did nothing to remind him of it. The problem went away, but my grandfather's lesson stayed with me forever.

One thing I loved while growing up was hearing my grandfather play music. My mom and I would visit my grandparents every Saturday evening for dinner. When we were at their home in Oak Park, I would beg him to play his silver trumpet. He would buzz his lips a few minutes before playing. Once he began to blow sounds from his horn, I would sit in amazement. For more than 40 years, my grandfather carried his trumpet around like it was a sword. He played in several jazz bands and even recorded an album before he entered the service. Every morning before dawn, he would sit on his porch and play improvised tunes. Since there weren't any roosters on the West

Side of Chicago, he provided a morning wake-up call for all of his neighbors. He once told me that the trumpet was his first love because it talked only when he wanted it to. I didn't get the joke until later, but it showed me how much he cared for the instrument and his music.

When I was 9 years-old, I lost my best friend. My grandfather went to sleep one night and never woke up. His funeral was held on a dreary spring day at Landmark Missionary Baptist Church. I held back my tears because I figured he would be disappointed if I didn't stand strong. He would always tell me, "Be a man for your momma." And at that moment, I wanted to show everyone that I could be as strong a man as he was. I could have used his guidance as I got older, but I was lucky to be able to spend my first nine years with him.

A couple of days after his death, my grandmother handed me the greatest gift that I have ever received. It was my grandfather's silver trumpet. I held the instrument in my hands for several minutes and examined its features.

My grandfather would sometimes allow me to play with his trumpet and taught me how to blow a couple of notes. I was far from even being an average horn player for my age, so I thought about hanging it up on my wall as a reminder of him. My grandmother didn't like the idea and insisted that I play it. She gave me a mouthpiece that she bought from the music store and handed me my grandfather's favorite record, *Kind of Blue* by Miles Davis.

I studied that record as if I was going to be tested on it. Each note reminded me of the Saturday evenings when my grandfather put on old records and then played his horn. I attempted to copy my grandfather's routine by playing the record and then picking up the horn to mimic the melodies. The sounds that I played were so off-key that the neighbors would knock on the door and beg my mother to make me stop.

"Tina, you need to tell your son to stop playing that damn horn, it's irritating the hell out of us!"

"Please! We're trying to sleep over here."

"Somebody needs to shut that little boy up now!"

The neighbors never got to my mother. She would shrug them off and encourage me to continue with my noise. I'm sure that I also gave her headaches when I played, but she preferred that I made noise in the house rather than go outside and end up in trouble. I would blow into the horn until my jaws were sore. My mother bought tapes and a tape recorder so that I could record myself. The more I played, the better the notes began to sound. Years passed and I began to mirror some of the same sounds that emanated from the horn of Miles Davis. It took a while, but my progression at least shut the neighbors up.

The only time I put the horn down was to pick up a basketball. I fell in love with the game when I was 9 years-old. I remember watching Magic Johnson throw a no-look pass that was so incredible that I stared at the TV for at least one minute without blinking. The TV station replayed the pass several times and that was all I needed for inspiration. I grabbed my ball and tried hard to recreate that pass in the hallway outside my front door. I dribbled on the wooden floor and threw no-look passes against the wall.

Sometimes the no-look passes would hit the wall and bounce down the wooden steps that led to the entrance to my building. I would run as fast as I could to grab the ball and bring it back up the steps before it reached the front door. On one occasion, I lost control of the ball and it rolled all the way to the entrance.

I grabbed the ball and started to run back up the steps, but the sounds of children yelling and older dudes talking drew my attention. I wanted to see what was going on outside of that door.

I opened the door and stepped outside. Five teenagers were standing on the sidewalk talking and laughing while passing a smoldering brown wrinkled-looking cigar from one to the other. A couple of young girls played hop-scotch across the street. And three boys around my age were sitting on the red steps and talking to each other. There was a short kid who had on Pro Wing shoes, a t-shirt with a mixture of dirt and red soda on it, and hair that looked like a bucket of sand had been poured in it. The other kid was my height and chubby. He held a candy bar in his hand and wore a tight blue t-shirt that was too small to cover his stomach completely. The third kid was tall, with dark tone skin, an athletic build and thick eye-glasses.

The shortest kid looked at me and asked, "Where you stay at?" I turned around and pointed to my apartment. The chubby kid then asked, "How come we don't ever see you outside?" Those boys had probably played in the streets since they were four. Since I was nine years-old, I was already five years behind in relating to what went on outside of my mother's front door. But I didn't want them to know that I was such a rookie. So in an awkward voice I replied, "I don't come outside because I don't play!" All three of the boys looked at each other and then turned their heads back towards me.

The shortest boy challenged my statement by suggesting that we play a game that would test my fighting skills. In a raspy voice, the short kid looked at me and said, "Let's slap box." I turned to him and said, "Man, didn't I tell you that I don't play?" He responded by pushing me in the chest and calling me a punk. My heart pounded and my hands began to shake. The short kid walked onto the sidewalk, formed a fist and jumped up and down as if he were warming up for a prizefight. I placed my basketball on the stoop and walked down the red steps. I had not thought about using a left jab in a fight since the day after I was accused of stealing by Big Lenny Green. It was time for me to put everything that my grandfather had taught me to use.

I was scared but ready. Escaping this situation was not an option. This was something that I needed to go through to be accepted outside of my home. If I allowed this boy to punk me, I would never be able to step outside again without being picked on.

We stood eye-to-eye and neither one of us blinked. The short kid attacked first by slapping me clean on the jaw. I heard "oohs" as the older teens and kids in the neighborhood watched. But I was too much for him. Although the boy was determined to be the first person on the block to get the best of me, he soon found out that my arms were too long for him to compete. After taking a couple of hits, I began to hit him with a fury of slaps on both sides of his face. I felt as if I was conquering the world until the chubby boy grabbed me from behind and slammed me to the ground.

The neighborhood kids looked on and laughed. I attempted to stand up, but the chubby boy was too strong. Somehow, I squirmed out of his grasp and got on top of him. I placed my forearm on his neck and the short boy pushed me off of the chubby boy. While both the short and chubby boys tussled with me, the tall boy who wore glasses just looked on. Someone tugged my right arm and pulled me up. An older gray-haired man pulled us apart. As I got up from the ground I heard,

"Minus, get your butt in this house!" The neighborhood kids laughed louder as I wiped the dirt off of my clothes and walked back to my apartment breathing heavily while my mom stood at the top of the red steps with her arms folded.

After the fight, my mother put me on punishment and made sure that I was in the house and away from trouble. For several weeks, she would not allow me to play with my basketball in the hallway. My only activities were playing board games and practicing my horn. That kept me occupied only for a short time. The outside was just too intriguing for a curious nine year-old boy.

Two months of punishment did nothing to soften my hard-head. Once my mother lifted the restrictions and allowed me to go back to the hallway and play ball, I again found myself chasing the ball down the steps as my dribbling got away from me. I picked up the ball at the entrance and opened the door. I stepped outside and wanted to go farther than the red steps. I needed to see more of this place that was my neighborhood. The corner store down the street was my destination. My mother and I would often walk together to the corner store to pick up juice or snacks, but it seemed as if I was going there for the first time when I traveled alone.

Walking alone was freedom. It was amazing to see young girls jumping rope and counting to a beating rhythm while older men stood in groups talking and sipping from bottles covered by brown paper bags in their hands. The aroma of warm meat that seeped out of the stove of a mobile hot dog stand caused me to remember that I hadn't eaten in hours. As I continued, I saw older women slowly stepping off of the bus with bags full of groceries and two teeange boys tossing a football to each other. I was only minutes away from those red steps, but it felt as if I were discovering a new world for myself.

I arrived at the store and I heard a voice say, "Hey Joe, what's up?" I turned around and saw the tall boy with glasses who was sitting on my porch a couple of months earlier wearing a muddy gray jacket and a faded small gold chain around his neck. My palms began to sweat. I looked passed his shoulders to see if anyone was with him. I thought that he would try to finish what his other two friends had started, so I balled up my fist as he walked closer. If he wanted to fight me, I was going to prepare myself the best way that I knew how. But he stuck his hand out and gave me five as if we had hung tight the day before. Without telling me, I knew he was impressed by the way I handled myself against his boys. After a couple of minutes of small talk, I asked the dude, "What do they call you?" He looked at me for a few seconds and glanced inside of the store window and said, "Blue." He then turned and asked if I wanted anything from the store. Before he walked inside, I told him, "Naw, I'm cool."

I sat on the edge of the curb and absorbed what was going on in my neighborhood. Being in the outside world by myself gave me a feeling of independence. I could have sat on that sidewalk all day and observed the cars and people walking by. However, I abruptly discovered that I would have to discover my neighborhood on another day.

Blue dashed out of the store. His hands were full and two candy bars fell out of his pockets as the storeowner hurried behind him. Without giving it a second thought, I ran. I was afraid that the storeowner would grab me and ask questions about Blue. Sitting down and answering questions about a dude who I knew little about would waste too much time considering that I had to be back in that hallway before my mom opened the front door. So without hesitation, I sprinted from the corner store and continued running until I reached those bright red steps.

By the time I turned 11 years-old, my mother loosened her grip and allowed me to play outside until the street lights hit the pavement. She also began to work more hours, so I had more time to discover things for myself. Being outside helped me to understand the streets and what was going on in my neighborhood. I soon realized that being on those sidewalks, even to play ball, was a privilege and not a right.

I can recall one summer afternoon when a boy my age named Calvin walked outside holding a polish sausage that he bought from Jew Town. During the summer, the only kids who ate in the afternoon were the ones who stole from the store or scraped pennies together to buy candy or chips. So we would all play hard in the heat of the summer with stomachs so empty that the only thing we could taste on our tongues was the salt from the sweat that poured down our faces. My grandmother used to tell me that a person should never walk outside and eat in front of friends unless he had enough to feed the entire neighborhood. Calvin learned that lesson the hard way.

A few of the guys in the neighborhood were playing baseball on the street when Calvin showed up with a polish sausage in his hand. Fat Nate, the chubby kid who I fought with on my first day outside, asked Calvin for a piece of sausage. Calvin decided to continue to eat the sausage around hungry boys without sharing. He looked at Fat Nate and told him, "No." Fat Nate said, "Ight," and turned his back as if he was walking away. Fat Nate took one step forward, then turned back around and punched Calvin square on the nose. Calvin grabbed his nose and Fat Nate slapped the polish sausage out of his hand and stepped on it. Fat Nate walked away and laughed.

Fat Nate was the bully of the neighborhood. He talked mounds of trash and punked whoever would back down when he got in their face. If he sensed fear in the person who stood before him, he wouldn't hesitate to push, slap or punch them without reason. But he never confronted or messed with Blue. For some reason, Fat Nate made it a point to talk to Blue with respect. I could never figure it out, but Fat Nate's entire demeanor changed when Blue was around.

Blue began to stop by my house more often. I think he liked the fact that I stood my ground and did not try too hard to prove myself. He introduced me to most of the boys around the neighborhood and those who stayed in the Dearborn projects. Although Blue and I were friends, it took a while for me to earn respect from the other boys in Dearborn. That was, until I discovered they all liked to flip backwards. Doing a backwards flip was a rite of passage. Most of the Dearborn boys would practice flipping backwards for days on the grass and on old mattresses. It took weeks and months for some of the boys to learn how to do a backward flip. I attempted my first backward flip on a patch of grass. With Blue and about eight boys standing around me, I jumped straight backwards and landed on my feet without stumbling. From that day on, I was accepted in Dearborn.

As Blue and I got older, we became hanging partners around the neighborhood. We were brothers from different mothers. Most of the people who stayed in our area believed we were cousins, but we didn't share an ounce of family blood.

Blue and his baby sister, India, stayed with his grandmother in the Dearborn projects. His 24 year-old cousin Andrea, and her three kids, would stay at the apartment for months at a time.

Andrea had her own issues to deal with, so Blue's grandmother was forced to take care of him and his sister alone. But Blue's grandmother could barely keep up with his whereabouts, so he took on the challenge of raising himself and living by his own rules.

I later found out the reason that he and the other two boys were sitting on my apartment steps on the day of my first fight. Once the Dearborn dealers began to sell drugs in front of my building, they would recruit young boys like Blue and Fat Nate to serve as watch-outs when the police arrived. They figured that the younger boys could camouflage themselves as regular kids outside playing. But Blue wanted to be more than a watch-out man — he wanted to own the block.

Blue stopped serving as watch-out and began committing random crimes whenever he saw an opportunity. While hanging with Blue and the other boys from Dearborn, I saw things that the average person my age didn't. By the time I was 12, I had already seen several guns and small sacks of crack and weed. I knew that Blue was into some foul things, but we were boys. So I never looked at him sideways for what he showed me and some of the things that he did.

On a warm summer night in 1986, Blue and I were walking down West 27th when he noticed that someone left their keys in the ignition of a white Buick. Bold at the age of 12, Blue jumped behind the wheel of the car like it was his. Blue shut the car door, turned the key in the ignition and looked at me and said, "You riding?" I hesitated for three seconds and opened the passenger door.

We cruised through the South Side like we were the mayors of Chicago. It was the ultimate high to travel around the block, not walking or riding a bike. We had the transportation, but we needed a place to go. "Let's drive to McGuane Park, all the girls over there like dudes with rides," I said. "Naw man. I'm going to pick Tanisha up. I know she gonna be all over me now that I got this car," Blue shouted back.

"It's passed that girl's bedtime. Turn on the radio, let's see what these speakers sound like." I turned up the stereo to its highest decibel as Doug E. Fresh and Slick Rick blasted on the radio. "Minus, you wanna get behind this wheel and drive?"

"Yeah, pull over and let me take it." Blue slowed down on East 31st Street and a cop's car turned behind us. I told Blue to keep driving at the same pace and not to look in his rearview mirror. The last thing we needed was to go down to the Cook County jail. But he panicked. Blue put more pressure on the gas pedal and clutched the steering wheel tighter. He made a quick right turn and lost control. The car jumped the curve and slammed into a fire hydrant.

We both rushed to open the car doors and ran our separate ways. I took my shirt off and threw it to the side of me. I ran behind an apartment and hid in a small alley off of South State Street. After running and hiding for about 20 minutes, I decided to go home. I was relieved to finally be back on West 27th Street, until I saw a police car pass me slowly. I put my head down and continued to walk at a steady pace. I lifted my head slightly and noticed that Blue was in the back of the squad car. Blue looked me in the eye and didn't say a word. He could have snitched at that very moment, but he remained quiet.

Blue was charged with auto theft, but because of his age, he only served one week in a detention center for juveniles. At the tender age of 12, I had my first brush with the law. But it would not be the last.

CHAPTER 2

They were not just shoes; they were JORDANS. —Minus Hall

"Money, it's gotta be the shoes!"

I will never forget the first time I saw Michael "Money" Jordan and Spike Lee, I mean Mars Blackmon, in that famous 1988 commercial. The moment that commercial aired, I knew I would walk in those shoes one day. The sight of "Money" dunking the ball in an empty gym while Mars Blackmon yelled in the black and white 30-second piece was mesmerizing. The black leather shoes had a black and gray elephant print trim on the side, an air bubble on the white sole, and a red Jumpman emblem stitched on top of the shoe's black tongue. There was nothing like it in the world.

Since the day MJ was drafted by the Bulls as the third pick in 1984, Chicago has never been the same. A larger-than-life black hero had finally landed in my city. Magic Johnson was cool, but in the Chi, MJ was the man. We all thought of him as our salvation. Jesus hadn't come, but MJ was sure to drop 50 on any given night.

The swagger. The walk. The long shorts. The baldhead. The tongue. MJ was more than a basketball player, he was a mixture of sports, the streets and greatness. Standing at only 6-foot-6, he played as if he was nine feet tall. When he walked on the court, he intimidated every player on the court not wearing his uniform. Players tried double-teaming him, triple-teaming him, and knocking the hell out of him when he went to the basket for a lay-up. But hitting him hard did nothing. It fueled him. The harder he was hit, the higher he jumped, the farther he flew. You knew there was no way you could ever be as good as him, so you conceded to his greatness and tried hard as hell to be just like him.

During the `80s, Chicago playgrounds were full of MJ wanna-bes that ran up and down the court like cheap facsimiles of the real thing. Street ball players with wristbands on their left elbows stuck out their tongues while holding an arch in their right hand and attempted the trademark fade away that MJ perfected.

While fades and box haircuts were the style of the late`80s, Chicagoans ignored contemporary fashion and wore baldheads to show respect for Mike. And although Kojak allowed some dudes to feel comfortable wearing a baldhead, MJ damn near made it a requirement.

And then there were the shoes. The shoes were another effect of his greatness. An item created for his signature style that became available to the public. They were bought and worn as a symbol of superiority. They were not just shoes; they were JORDANS. We called them J's or 23s around my way. To tie those shoes on your feet meant that you were attaching yourself to something as valuable as real estate. For any black teenager in Chicago, having 23s was equivalent to having a car, or even a house. And since there was not a good chance that I, or any other teen on the South Side could afford a car or house, 23s were the next best thing.

A year before that commercial aired, I got a chance to see the Air J's number II in person for the first time. During the times that Blue and I met in Dearborn, we would walk to the basketball court and sit on the sidelines as the older guys shot ball for money. The older guys rarely ran whole court games. Instead, the best shooters in Dearborn shot three-pointers for the money that the dope dealers put up.

A dude name Clutch was probably the best shooter on the entire South Side of Chicago. He was a 5-foot-11, 18-year-old who had a jump shot that was out of this world. They called him Clutch because if he had the ball in the clutch situations of a game, he was sure to make the shot. Whenever the guys decided to play whole court games in Dearborn, Clutch would pull up from almost half court and hit all-net shots. He could practically shoot with his eyes closed and make the shot from anywhere on the court. There was a rumor in Dearborn that Clutch went to the legendary Franklin Park and dropped 40 points on an NBA player during a pick-up basketball game. Clutch probably could have gone to the NBA himself, but the streets drafted him first.

The day Blue and I walked to the Dearborn basketball court in late April of 1987, dollar bills covered the half-court circle like leaves in the middle of autumn. The dealers placed $10, $20 and $50 bills on the court as Clutch shot jumpers against another Dearborn resident, Breeze. They both shot jumpers for $50 on each made shot. While most of the money was on Clutch, that day Breeze was lucky. He hit every three-point jumper while the usually sure-handed Clutch missed shot after shot. By the end of their game, Clutch owed Breeze more than $1100. Clutch handed Breeze $600. He explained to Breeze that he didn't have any more money. Breeze then pointed to Clutch's shoes. Clutch took off the all-white shoes that had black shoestrings and all-black soles. He pulled up his socks and reluctantly handed the shoes to Breeze.

Green to the entire situation, I looked at Blue and asked, "Man why would Breeze want his shoes? Clutch has already worn them."

Blue looked at me with his nose turned up and said, "Minus, do you know what just happened? Breeze just got $600 from Clutch, and he took his new 23s. Everybody wants those sneaks!" At that time, I knew about the greatness of Michael Jordan the player, but the prominence of his shoes in the streets was new to me. However, it didn't take long for me to catch on.

Seven months after seeing Breeze accept a pair of shoes in exchange for cash due, I went to my mom and asked her to buy me those shoes for Christmas. I was beginning to understand why wearing those shoes was so important. MJ was the best. And if you were lucky enough to have his shoes, you were damn near the best.

"Mom, you know I just made an 80 on my last Math test," I said in an attempt to soften her up while she sat in her favorite chair watching *The Cosby Show*.

"That's good, honey," she said. "You need to keep up the good work."

"Christmas is almost here and I don't really want that much this year."

"Really?" she asked while continuing to watch as the Huxtable's plot unfolded.

"All I really want is some shoes."

"Alright, what kind do you want?"

"Some Jordans," I replied with excited coolness.

"Jordoons? Alright, I'll see what I can do."

The next day after middle school let out, Blue and I caught the bus to our friend Larry's house. Larry was one of the few people I knew who lived with both of his parents. His family lived in a modest house with four bedrooms and two bathrooms off Lakeshore Drive. His father was a detective for the Chicago Police Department and his mother was a nurse at the same hospital where my mom worked. Larry was the "Ricky" of my crew. He wasn't nearly as rich as Ricky from *Silver Spoons*, but his folks seemed to be doing better than most of our parents. Larry was always the first to get the things that everyone else wanted. He owned a go-cart, a BMX 10-speed bike, and nearly every game that came out on Nintendo and Sega. Larry also had a basketball hoop in his driveway.

On weekends and some days after school, my friends Peanut, Calvin and Meathead would join Larry, Blue and I to play 21 or 3-on-3 basketball games. Meathead was the clown of the group. The boys in the neighborhood gave him the nickname because of his large oval shaped head and pudgy neck. Not much time passed when he wasn't yapping or telling jokes.

Meathead also had a reputation for being a serial hater. He found reasons to hate on anyone breathing within his vicinity. If someone made a shot during a basketball game, he would say, "Aww man, that shot ain't nothing. I could've made that." If one of us got with a girl he would say, "Man she ain't all that. I've been with chicks that look a whole lot better than her." And the day I told my boys that I was getting the new 23s, he continued to do what he did best — discount it.

As Blue, Larry, Meathead, Peanut, Calvin and I played a game of 21 in Larry's driveway, I broke the news.

"Guess what. I'm getting those new 23s for Christmas," I said with confidence as if they were already on my feet.

"Joe, you're not getting those 23s," Meathead replied.

"Who's going to pay for`em? You don't have a job."

"Do what I do. I'll just take `em from a bastard," Blue said as all of us laughed.

"Man those new shoes are bad. But you know he's coming out with the number III's in February. Why don't you wait until then to get `em?" Larry asked.

"My change is strange right now and the only times that my mom would think about buying me some shoes is for the first day of school and Christmas. I have to get these shoes now or never. I've been working my ass off at the house, so I'm giving her a reason to have them under the tree on Christmas morning," I replied while dribbling the basketball. Meathead interrupted and presented me with a challenge.

"Minus, I bet a meal that you won't get those 23s for Christmas," he said. All of my boys looked at me to see if I would punk out. I stuck out my pinky finger, locked it with his, and while looking directly at him I said, "That's a bet."

As Meathead and I locked pinky fingers, Larry's father walked outside and asked us what all the commotion was about. Detective Murray stood a few inches under 6-feet and had a pot belly that seemed to get larger by the day. He usually wore dull-colored suits and brim hats over his short afro. On that day, he wore jogging pants and a yellow and blue PAL t-shirt. I passed him the basketball and he began to shoot with us. Blue hated cops, but Detective Murray was so cool that he didn't view him as an enemy with a gold badge. He was probably the only cop that Blue could be around for more than five minutes without being irritated by the sight and smell of police.

"So Mr. Murray, what you think about MJ?" Blue asked Detective Murray.

"He's pretty good."

"Pretty good? MJ got the NBA on lock. He makes grown men run like little girls," Peanut added.

"He's good for today's standards. Back when I was coming up, we had some real ball players. First there was the Big O. Oscar Robertson. He averaged a triple-double during an entire season. That's 30 points, 12 rebounds, and about 11 assists. Then there was big Wilt "The Stilt" Chamberlain. Now he really made grown men run. He averaged 50 points per game during a season and scored 100 points in one game. MJ hasn't come close to doing that. He and Scottie have brought some much needed energy to this city, but I think he still has to do more to be as good as the guys who played when I was your age."

Detective Murray shot the ball and it bounced off the backboard. He asked for the ball again and hit his second shot attempt. Before walking back inside his home, he told Larry that our game would have to end as soon as their porch light came on.

"No disrespect Larry, but I think your dad needs to stick to arresting people. He doesn't know too much about basketball," Meathead said after Detective Murray closed the back door.

"The truth is that MJ is the man right now," Larry said. "He's putting up major points on the court. And if you can get your hands on those shoes, you're gonna put up major points on the block *and* with all the girls."

From that day on, I continued to talk about the shoes around my mom. She usually nodded in agreement just so I would shut up. But she soon found a way to make my desire work in her favor. She used it as leverage to get me to do odd chores around our apartment. After I finished my homework on school nights, I swept the floor, washed the dishes and cleaned the house until she could give the countertops the white glove test. The work was boring and exhausting, but I was sure that my house chores would all pay off on Christmas morning.

Christmas on Chicago's South Side was merry to some, and just another day to most. Some of my friend's mothers would scrape enough money together to buy presents for them even if they were struggling to pay bills. That meant selling food stamps for cash, having bake sales, or saving what little they could from their pay-checks.

I didn't have a lot growing up, but my mom did her best to take care of me. Even when things were bad during the year, she always found a way to place a present for me under the tree on Christmas morning. The Christmas of 1987 was no different. For weeks, I stared at the box that was gift wrapped under the tree. The box was proof that she kept her promise of buying the 23s that I wanted so badly. I couldn't wait to open the box, lace up the shoes and run to Meathead's house and watch his reaction when he saw the real deal on my feet.

During most Christmas holidays, our cousins from Mississippi would visit. My mom was close to her first cousin Lucille. They were the same age and spent summers together when they were younger. Lucille had two kids named Howard and Samantha. Howard was three years younger than me and a rising star on his little league football team in Jackson. His mother would always brag to me about how he performed during the season.

"You know Minus, Howard scored 12 touchdowns this

season. His team even won the city's youth championship. They were all in the newspaper and stuff. Minus, when are you gonna start playing football?" she asked.

"We really don't play football that much around here. I'm down with the Chicago Bears, but most of my friends play basketball," I answered.

"Oh," she said with the disappointment of a Southerner who viewed football as the most important thing behind God, food and shelter. Samantha was three years older than me and talked about her boyfriend every chance that she got.

"Minus, you kinda look like that boy from New Edition," Samantha said.

"Who? Ronnie? Bobby? Ralph?" I asked as she looked at me and sketched out my facial features.

"No, Ricky. You're brown-skinned and have eyes just like him. Your ears stick out a little bit, and if you had an S-Curl in your box haircut, you would look just like him. How tall are you?"

Samantha asked while looking at the top of my head as if she was trying to figure out my height by guessing.

"I'm about 5'7."

"My boyfriend Jeffrey starts on our high school basketball team. He's already 6-foot-1. How much do you weigh?"

"I don't know, I guess about 165."

"Oh. Jeffrey weighs 180 pounds, but he has more muscles."

"I'd have more muscles if I lifted pigs and cows on the farm every day."

"Whatever Minus. That's why I couldn't stay up here in Chicago. It is way too cold! Plus Jeffrey don't stay here."

That Christmas, I heard the name Jeffrey so much that I would not have been surprised if she said that he was Jesus' nephew. It continued when she asked what I was getting for Christmas.

"Minus, what do you think your momma got you for Christmas?" Samantha asked as she played UNO in my room with Howard and me.

"She probably got me those 23s," I answered.

"23s! What are those?" She asked with her eyebrows twisted.

"Air Jordans," Howard clarified for her.

"Jeffrey told me that Michael Jordan's middle name was Jeffrey. But Michael Jordan don't look nearly as good as my Jeffrey."

Samantha ran her mouth about Jeffrey until she talked herself to sleep. She slept in my bed, and Howard and I put a few pillows together and slept on the floor. But I stayed up all night thinking about what the 23s would look like on me. I wanted to know how they would feel when I slid them on. I couldn't wait to open the box, take the brown paper out of the shoes and lace the shoestrings.

On Christmas morning, we all woke up around 8 a.m. and gathered around our Christmas tree in the living room. Since they were our guests, my mom allowed Lucille, Samantha and Howard to open their presents first. As they shredded the gift-wrap from their presents, I continued to wait patiently while staring at the box that had red gift-wrap and a note that read *To: Minus, From: Mommy*. I smiled inside and my eyes glowed with excitement. I was preparing to give her a hug and a kiss on the cheek. Howard and Samantha opened their last gifts and I grabbed my only gift. I snatched the scotch tape from the edges and tore off the red gift-wrap. The shoebox looked strange. I took the top off of the box and could not believe what was inside.

"What is this?" I asked my mother.

"What is what?" she replied.

"Oh, them don't look like no J's Minus," Samantha stated adding in her two cents.

"I wanted 23s, not L.A. Gears."

"You better be glad I bought you those. I went to the store and saw how much those Jorans, Jorbans, or whatever you call them things, cost. And there's no way I'm spending $100 to buy you some darn shoes that you're going to get dirty anyway. You must have lost your mind!"

After the winter break, I returned to school wearing blue and white L.A. Gears. True, they were new shoes, but they were not 23s. During the school day, I attempted to dodge all of my boys by waiting until the halls were emptied before going to my next class. Once it was time for lunch, I avoided going to the cafeteria and sat in the back of the library. Most of my boys would never skip lunch to chill in a quiet place filled with books, so I knew that I would be safe there. I remained low-key for the first half of the school day. But before my last period class began, the plan went wrong. I took a swallow from the water fountain and turned when I heard snickering behind me. Meathead and Larry were both looking at my shoes as I wiped water off of my chin.

"What's going on Minus?" Meathead asked while laughing with his hand over his mouth.

"Where are the 23s Minus?" Larry asked.

"Oh, those are 23s. I think they're the L.A. version." Meathead chimed in.

"Yeah, let's see how far these L.A.'s can jump inside your

Chicago asshole," I shot back at Meathead.

"I'll tell you what," said Meathead. "After school, we can go to Mickey D's and you can buy me a meal and I'll call it even."

They both laughed and walked away. I turned and headed to my last period class knowing that I had to find a way to get those shoes. There was no way that I was going to go another year without having those 23s on my feet.

CHAPTER 3

We're scared to let people see us hurt or living without. -Hassan Wright

My only goal the following summer was to earn enough money to buy a pair of 23s. During the humid days in June, I walked through the city with the hopes of finding a job at a restaurant, clothing shop or grocery store.

The first store I applied at was Ridge's Souvenir Shop on Lakeshore Drive.

Ridge's sold post cards, coffee mugs, T-shirts and Chicago memorabilia. Selling T-shirts and coffee mugs seemed like an easy way to earn a few bucks without needing too much work experience. A small bell was attached to the glass door and rung when I walked through the entrance.

"May I help you?" I turned to my right and saw a short Korean woman standing behind the cash register.

"Yeah, um. I mean yes. I'm looking for work during the summer while I'm out of school and I wanted to know if…"

"I'm sorry. We're not looking for any workers right now."

"Well, can I at least fill out an application just in case you get an opening later?"

"I don't think we will be hiring anytime soon."

I applied at eight stores that day and the response was always the same. It seemed that boys my age were not ideal employees. I think employers believed that we would steal from the business, show up late for work or not show up at all. So instead of taking a chance on hiring someone who looked like me, the businesses preferred to give their current employees overtime. It was a messed up situation, but I had to make money somehow.

After two weeks of applying at grocery stores, newsstands and fast food restaurants without luck, I decided my appearance was part of the reason that I was still unemployed. I usually wore sweat pants, white T-shirts and tennis shoes. My box hair cut was turning into an Afro as the sides of my fade had grown out completely. I didn't have enough money to buy new dress clothes, but I could sometimes bum seven dollars from my mother to get a haircut. On a Thursday morning before she walked to work, my mother gave me a $20 loan and I caught the bus on South MLK Dr. to find a barbershop.

The bus drove 15 blocks south and I got off near a small shopping plaza that had several stores that included Mitchell's Clothing and a barbershop. A polish sausage stand was located in front of the plaza, so I decided to grab a grape soda and a bite to eat. As I approached the stand, a pearl white 1988 BMW 735i with limo tint windows parallel parked near the sidewalk. A tall brown-skinned man in his mid-20s stepped out of the car wearing a thick, dope gold chain, a blue and white leather Gucci suit, and the red, white, blue and gray number III edition of 23s. Before walking inside Mitchell's, he stopped and waved at someone inside the barber shop next door. Two other guys stepped out of the BMW. One of the men followed the man into the store, while the other guy stood in front of the store with his hands near his waist. From the way he carried himself, I could tell that the man in the Gucci suit owned his reality. It had to be a powerful experience to walk in his shoes.

Once the man entered Mitchell's, I focused my attention on the barbershop next door. I glanced at the red and blue sign that read "Lil D's Barber Shop" and peeked through the large glass window that was hedged by black burglar bars. There were seven occupied barber chairs and about 10 guys waiting for haircuts. From past experience, a full barbershop was a sign that a couple of the barbers could cut hair without leaving gashes on the sides of their client's head.

I walked into the barbershop and immediately found that most of the men in the shop were in the middle of a heated discussion. The customers and barbers all spoke louder than each other, in what seemed like a desperate effort to be heard. And the few who didn't have anything to say laughed louder than those who were talking. The chatter and laughter created a noise that was more constant than the buzzing of seven electric clippers. Nearly all of the barbers were engaged in conversations, so I walked over to the only one who wasn't talking and asked how many heads were in front of me. The slim, light-skinned guy wore a goatee, a barber's apron and a white beanie on his head. He held up his index finger and continued cutting.

Fifteen minutes passed before the barber looked at me and brushed hair off of the seat. I sat down in the black leather barber's chair and told him how I wanted my box cut while he tied an apron around my neck. Most of the barbers hung pictures of their love ones or girls in bikinis on the large mirror on the wall behind their chairs. A copy of a speech titled, "Harpers Ferry," by W.E.B DuBoise, was taped on the upper right side of the mirror behind the barber who cut my hair.

"So what's your name young brother?" The barber asked as he began cutting my hair.

"Minus," I replied.

"Minus. That's an interesting name. What school do you go to?"

"I just finished the eight grade, but I'll be going to Dunbar High in the fall."

"Paul Laurence Dunbar," the barber stated. "He was one of the greatest poets to ever walk on American soil. My favorite poem that he wrote was this piece called *We Wear The Mask.*"

"Don't think I ever heard of that one. What is it about?"

"It's about how we walk through life and shield ourselves from the truth. We're scared to let people see us hurt or living without. So every day we put on clothes, smiles and facades of happiness when we're really torn up inside. But once you know yourself and you're comfortable with yourself, that mask is no longer needed."

I passed that high school almost every day of my life, but I never thought about the person for whom it was named. I'm sure there were students who did not think, or even care about the great works that were written by the person whose name was on the front of their high school building.

"I've never heard of a name like Hassan. Are you from Africa or something?" I asked.

"No, young brother," he replied with a hint of laughter. "I grew up in the Robert Taylor Homes. I used to run with a group of guys when I was about your age or even younger. We were into the streets real heavy, but it eventually caught up with me at the age of 21. I was shot three times in a shoot out. I'm lucky to be here right now. But, while I was in the hospital, I decided that I needed to make some changes in my life. So a few months after I was shot, I stopped hanging around the old neighborhood and began studying business at the University of Chicago. During my first semester, I met someone who introduced me to the teachings and I changed my name."

Hassan said that he changed his first name because it gave him a sense of having a new beginning. It was like starting over from birth and becoming something other than what everyone else knew him as. But he said changing his name meant nothing without changing his way of thinking and actions. So he read more and hung out less. In his readings, he said that he discovered a lot about the world around him.

"The majority of people in our community have not been educated on how to live a correct life," Hassan said as he changed clippers.

"We've been made to believe that temporary satisfaction is the key to happiness, so we fall victim to having shortsighted goals. That's why you see old men sitting on corners drinking beer in the middle of the day instead of working. The stress of our environment has caused some good people to run from their situations by smoking crack and using heroin. These people can't raise their kids, so the young ones grow up having to figure it out by themselves. By the time the young ones get your age, they've been through so much out here that they become numb to the destruction that awaits them. So they waste their lives by looking for a high and sleeping until the weekend. We believe that having a good Saturday solves every problem. It's the only time that we can smile hard enough to keep from crying. Our constant chase to experience some type of high is just a reaction from us being low.

And the reason why we're low is because everything around here causes us to think low of ourselves. Liquor stores, slum housing and fast-food restaurants surround us. But we're bigger than where we are. We shouldn't have to seek poisons that give us artificial happiness and destroy us at the same time."

Listening to Hassan speak caused me to think about myself and what I saw going on outside of my home every day. It was strange to hear a person under 30 talking the way Hassan did. I was used to hearing dudes his age and younger talk about chicks, money, weed and clothes. He was the first person I met who gave reasons for why we chased those things. And in a sense, besides Detective Murray, he was the first positive talking man who I had met since my granddad passed.

After Hassan finished cutting my hair, I gave him $10 and asked if he knew of anyone that was hiring for a summer job. He told me he would ask around. We gave each other five and I walked out with a fresh haircut and a mini-lesson about life.

I caught up with Blue later that day in the Dearborn Housing projects. My first visit to Dearborn occurred in 1986, and two years later, it was a different place. The playground that was full of swings, sliding boards and monkey bars for children to play on, had become stations for dope dealers to sit as they made sales. The basketball court, which was once a place for the best ball players in Dearborn to show off their skills, was now infested with garbage, empty dime bags and graffiti. The only reminder that basketball had ever been played at that court was two white metal backboards without rims.

Blue sat on top of a green wooden bench in the courtyard

behind his building, 2971. He wore new Cazal glasses, a Chicago Bulls Starters hat, and a white t-shirt. He handed something to a hype as I approached. The hype grabbed the small item from Blue and clutched it tightly in his palms and walked away fast. Blue looked at me and nodded upward. Another hype approached him and asked if he could get some rocks on credit. Blue stood up from the bench and pushed the tall skinny man that wore a dingy black basketball jersey and dirt-stained jeans. Blue pushed the man again. The man, who stood a little over 6-feet, fell to the ground as Blue coughed up phlegm and spit it at him. Blue kicked the man in his stomach and said, "Get out of my face fool!" Blue turned around, sat back on the bench and gave me five as if nothing happened.

"Say Joe, you still trying to get a job? I see that you cut that bush off," Blue said while turning his head to see if anyone was approaching.

"Yeah man, these folks don't wanna hire a young cat like myself," I answered back.

"Man, you better get out here with me. These rocks is keeping my pockets healthy. Hypes be buying and come back in like 15 minutes begging for more. I ain't rich, but I got more than enough to eat," Blue said as he showed me a wad of money with a rubber band tied tightly around it. "Naw, I'm not ready to get out here yet. But if these jobs keep tripping ..." I responded as another hype ran up and handed Blue money.

"This here is going so good I don't think I'm gonna mess with school this year."

"So you finished with it? We're just now making it to high school. There's no telling what can happen."

"Man, ain't nothing gonna happen but a waste of time. While y'all in there faking like y'all learning, I'm gonna be out here earning. Besides, look at Tony over there. He graduated last year and couldn't find a job nowhere. So now he wanna come out here and make money. If he wouldn't have wasted his time by going to that crappy school, he might have a little something by now. But he out here trying to play catch up. That won't be me."

I knew that Blue would never walk into another school building again. I could have tried to talk him out of it, but when Blue made his mind up about something, it was usually written in concrete. We talked for a few more minutes before the hype traffic became too heavy for us to hold a conversation. I threw up a peace sign and headed home.

Before walking off, I turned and observed the buyers and sellers that were in the project's courtyard. The courtyard operated like a mini flea market. The dope dealers sold to the hypes, the hypes sold stolen TVs and VCRs to residents for as little as five dollars, and the money recycled itself like a bad cold.

Considering what I was going through to find a job, I began to understand why boys around my age dealt drugs. It was work for the poor and unemployed. Where else could a 14 year-old black male make hundreds of dollars in one day? The few opportunities that business owners gave black males caused us to expect rejection whenever we filled out an application. But providing for the hypes created income while the Chicago job market made it a point to be unforgiving.

But it was still illegal. At 14 years-old, I didn't want my first job to consist of watching out for the stick-up boys, cops and the snitching drug dealers who were quick to point fingers at their own co-workers just to get themselves out of trouble. It was a risky business in an area of the city where it was a risk to even walk outside. I didn't need that extra mark on me. So I decided to play it straight, at least for the time being.

I returned to Lil D's Barber Shop two weeks later to talk with Hassan about leads on jobs around the city. When I walked into the shop, I noticed cut hair and dirt scattered on the floor. The barbers were so busy that they rarely had time to sweep and keep the place clean. So I decided to present Hassan with a business proposition that would put money in my pocket and keep the floors of the barbershop clean. Hassan agreed that it would be a good idea, but he needed to ask the owner, Lil D before he could give me the OK.

I stuck around until closing time to talk with Lil D. Lil D appeared to be in his late forties. He stood about 5-foot-6, sported a box haircut with an S-curl, had a gold tooth with a "D" engraved in it and he often wore bright colored button-up shirts, Gucci slippers, leather shorts and long church socks that stopped just below his knees. After his last cut, Hassan introduced me to him.

"So you wanna work, huh?" Lil D asked in a rough voice, ravaged by years of drinking hard liquor.

"Yeah, I'm looking for a summer job."

"Well, what can you do? Can you cut hair?"

"No."

"Can you wash hair?"

"Nope."

"Can you do nails? I'm just pulling your shoestring young snapper. Hassan says that you want to keep the place clean. I can pay you about $10 a day to sweep and wipe off the counters. Just don't break nothing. If you break something, it's coming out of your paycheck. I need you here Monday through Saturday from 9:00 a.m. until 8:00 p.m."

The money wasn't great, but at $10 a day I would make $60 in six days of work. By the time school started, I had a chance to save about $200. And that was enough money to buy a few t-shirts and the new 23s.

Although it was work, I never thought of the barbershop as a job. It was more like attending an event. I would sit back and listen to the barbers and customers argue about sports, politics, neighborhood issues and women.

Lil D always played the bad guy, or the person who would disagree just for the sake of having an argument. I soon found out that the "D" stood for Detroit, a city hated by any Chicago sports fan. He opened the shop after leaving Detroit in the late 1970s, and he made sure that every person in the barbershop knew where he was from. His hatred for anything dealing with Chicago always created a stir in the barbershop. One day, the conversation got so heated that it almost ended with blows being thrown.

"I'm gonna tell y'all one thing. Jordan ain't never winning a championship in Chicago. The boy shoots too much, he never passes, and every time he plays my Detroit Pistons, we knock him right on his butt," Lil D shouted as the entire barbershop erupted.

Lil D knew how much we loved Jordan, but he continued to trash his name and other Chicago sports legends. "You see, MJ is a loser. I come from a winning city. The Michigan Wolverines won the Final Four, the Detroit Pistons just won the championship, and the Detroit Lions just got Barry Sanders. Give 'em some years and he's gonna be better than Walter Payton," Lil D said as he cleaned his clippers with a brush.

One man got so upset with Lil D that he gave him an invitation to leave the city. "If you hate Chicago so much, why don't you take your ass back to dirty ass Detroit!"

"Why don't you make me, punk," Lil D shot back. The guy, who was nearly 6-foot-3, got out of his seat and stood over Lil D. Lil D took off his barber's apron, placed his clippers on the counter, looked the guy in the eye and said, "Don't be stupid. You came in here alive, I'm sure you wanna leave out that way."

Hassan and the other barbers stepped between the two before anything serious could take place. After a while, it was commonplace for the heated conversations to almost boil over into a physical altercation.

While their conversations on sports were interesting, I always listened closely when they discussed women. Lil D, as usual, led the conversation.

"See y'all young boys don't know how to keep these ladies happy. All y'all wanna do is have fun and sleep. And then you wonder why she don't call you back no more," Lil D said.

Irv, a barber in his early 20s, disagreed with Lil D.

"Lil D, you're old school. These girls today don't want a man all up under them. If you get too attached, she knows that she got a sucker. And I ain't trying to let a chick get too attached to me, either. I'm dealing with too many to be stuck up under just one," Irv bragged while high-fiving the client who was in his chair.

"That's what I'm talking about. On Friday nights, I bet you go out with Nivea don't you?" Lil D asked Irv.

"Nivea? Who is Nivea?"

"Nivea lotion you right-handed hero. I bet you could

knock out Mike Tyson with your right hand," Lil D said as everyone in the barbershop erupted in laughter and pointed at Irv.

Irv put his head down and continued to cut his client's hair. Unable to top Lil D's taunt, Irv remained silent for the rest of the day.

Nearly three weeks after my first day of work at the barbershop, Blue stopped by on a Wednesday afternoon wearing a navy blue and gray Georgetown Hoyas Starter jacket, a matching Georgetown starter hat, and blue and white Cortez Nikes. I placed the broom and dustpan in the back of the barbershop and greeted Blue outside.

"I see the hustle ain't too bad, ha?" I nudged at Blue's shoulder to give props to his new gear.

"Boy you just don't know. So when they gonna start letting you cut hair in this spot?" Blue said while peeking inside of the shop.

"I'm trying to learn it. Some of these dudes knock out 30 heads in a day at $10 a pop. And the owner Lil D got his customers plus he's getting 15 percent booth rent from every barber in there."

"Guess it ain't too bad for the common man. So what's up Joe, you hungry? Let's go down to Army & Lou's and grab something to eat. It's on me."

"We can do that. Let me go inside and talk to Lil D so that he'll know I'm gone."

"Do your thing."

Blue and I walked down East 75th to Army & Lou's restaurant. Army & Lou's was one of the oldest black-owned restaurants in the Midwest and served the best soul food in Chicago. I ordered fried chicken wings, macaroni and cheese, sweet potato pie and grape soda. Blue got fried pork chops, dressing and collard greens. We sat down and discussed our summer jobs as we devoured our food.

"So how long you think you gonna be out there on the hustle?" I asked Blue before taking a sip of grape soda.

"With that, it's about how you work it. A lot of those boys at the hustle don't have a plan. And that's cool because it makes it that much easier for us that do. I'm putting together a team. Right now I'm still working out of Breeze's stash, but I got a few boys that's coming to me for work. I got Lil Lee, Young Phil and Fat Nate getting it from me and I should double my profit by the end of the summer," Blue responded before checking his beeper.

"What about the people you got working your stuff. You think they're gonna bring you all your money?"

"Everybody knows right from wrong, it just comes down to what side you wanna be on. If one of those boys get on the wrong side, it'll just give me more reason to do what I think is right."

"I see. But what else you gonna do with the money? It can't all be about work."

"Joe, you know we about to do it big. I talked to Larry a couple of days ago. He wants to get all the boys together to hit up Six Flags before the summer ends. Catch some of those North Side skirts in action. You gonna be down?"

"You know me. I'm with it."

We stumbled out of Army & Lou's with toothpicks in our mouths and full stomachs. But neither of us could afford to go home and sleep our meals off. The one-hour lunch break was over and we both had jobs to return to.

Weekdays at the barbershop were unlike the weekends. Only a few customers showed up during the week and it was easy for me to keep the shop clean from Monday through Thursday. The boredom was hard to shake on the slow days. So to help pass the time, I began to take my grandfather's trumpet to the barbershop, and I played outside once I finished cleaning.

Some of the younger barbers would call me 'Little Trumpet Boy' whenever I played. But I got the chance to laugh back as people walking by the barbershop would put tips in my hat while I blew my grandfather's horn. Along with the money Lil D paid me to sweep, I was beginning to make up to $30 a day with the extra tips.

Soon, my trumpet playing became an attraction to the barbershop. Small crowds would gather around me as I belted out the six songs from the Miles Davis album. Lil D began to encourage me to play more. He said my sidewalk concerts brought more customers to his shop. So like any smart businessman, I asked for a raise. Lil D hesitated at first, but he eventually agreed to add $5 to my weekly pay.

On a cloudy Tuesday afternoon in late July, I was blowing a tune when a white guy in his late 40s or early 50s stopped in front of the barbershop. The heavyset guy wore a black derby hat, a blue cotton shirt and his pants were held up by a belt that was buckled above his navel. Thin-framed glasses sat on the bridge of his nose and he held three albums under his right arm. He didn't appear to be an average spectator amused by the sight of a 14 year-old blowing a horn. Instead, he stared at the ground and listened as if he were studying every note that I played. The guy began to shake his head and closed his eyes as if he were being offered garbage.

"Um, why would you do that?" he asked as he lifted his

head and looked at me.

"Excuse me?" I asked while removing the horn from my mouth and looking back at the guy as if he had a serious problem.

"So What," the guy said as I stared at him with a confused look.

" 'So What.' " From the classic Mile Davis album, *Kind of Blue*," the guy clarified.

"Oh. Yeah, I like to play that song every now and then."

"I hear it, but I'm not hearing it."

"Old man, I don't know what you're talking about."

"Your notes. You're missing very important notes. To the virgin ear, what you're playing sounds OK. But to someone who knows how it's supposed to sound, that's a disgrace. See Miles told stories with the horn. Look at it as if you're building a house. You wouldn't build the first floor and then skip to the third. You would have to build the second floor. That's what you have to do when you're playing music."

"No offense, but I'm not really out here to be a music legend. I'm just trying to earn enough money to buy some new kicks."

"With what I'm hearing, under the right guidance, you might be able to earn enough money to buy more than shoes. What school do you go to?"

"I'm going to be in my first year at Dunbar next month."

"Do you play in the school's band?"

"Heck no. Does it look like I would hang around a bunch of corn balls who play in the band? Man what's up with all of these questions?"

"Well, my name is Thomas Peterson. I work in the music department at New Trier High School in Winnetka.

It's one of the most prestigious music schools in the country. Major colleges and universities award thousands of dollars in scholarships to our students each year. We also have a jazz band that travels around the country to perform in concerts."

"Winnetka? What are you doing down here on the South Side?"

"I just picked up a few tunes from the Jazz Record Mart and I'm now on my way to grab a bite to eat. I want you to take my business card. I think that you'd be a good addition to our program. I also think that our program would be a good addition for you."

The man handed me a business card and walked away. I placed the card in my back pants pocket and continued to play. Transferring to another school just to play the horn didn't mean much to me. I played the horn only because I wanted to. I wasn't going to let some old music teacher force me to play bullshit songs for his uppity school.

By the end of the summer, I had over $400 saved in my shoebox. Some of the money went towards helping my mother with the bills and I used $60 to pay for the trip that I took to Six Flags with Blue, Larry and the rest of my boys. I enjoyed the last days of August up until my time at the barbershop was over. I was upset that I could no longer work at the shop every day and listen to the guys go back and forth at each other on politics, sports, and women. I was also forced to give up earning extra dollars from playing my grandfather's horn. The start of fall usually marked the beginning of a new journey. My first year of high school was approaching and the summer heat was waning by the minute.

CHAPTER 4

He looked like a man who was satisfied with just being.
-Minus Hall

The bell rang 15 minutes after 8 a.m. at Paul L. Dunbar Vocational Career Academy. Security guards with guns in their holsters and metal detectors stood at the entrance as students rushed the door, eager to get into the 47-year-old school for the first day of the 1988-89 school year. "Welcome Freshmen Class of 1992" was printed on a large banner that hung in the main lobby. As each student entered, the security guards asked us to raise our hands so they could check for weapons by patting our arms, waists and legs. Book bags were also opened and looked through. One of the security guards sat at a table with a clipboard and white bucket to the side of her. I peeked inside the bucket and noticed that there were pocketknives, small cans of pepper spray attached to key chains and fingernail files. Once the security guards searched me, I grabbed my book bag and walked to the main hallway on the first floor.

The voices of over 1,000 teenagers echoed through the hallway as boys gave each other five and girls hugged each other. Most of the boys wore high top fades, starter jackets, Adidas, Nike Air Forces or the 23s that came out the year before. The upperclassmen leaned with their backs against the wall as if they owned real estate near the lockers. The boys leaning on the lockers were separated in groups. The athletes hung with the athletes, the thugs gathered with their pants sagging and bandannas tied around their heads, and the brainy kids had their own crew.

The girls were mind-blowing to a 14-year-old boy fresh out of the 8th grade. They weren't ashamed to show off their 17-and 18-year-old bodies in tight biking shorts that did justice to their teenage figures. Gold bamboo earrings hung from their earlobes while they talked through glossy lips. They wore finger waves, stacks and braids to stand out and make a statement. And they walked with a switch that said, "You can try, but I know you can't handle this."

I found myself on the outside of it all as a freshman. My first period class was World History, which was taught by a middle-aged woman named Ms. Foster. Ms. Foster wore small brown rimmed glasses, stood just over 5-feet tall, had a double chin that sagged near the top of her chest, and her blonde hair was beginning to gray. It was early in the school day and Ms. Foster's forehead was already moist with sweat. Her shouting at students who interrupted her lesson by chatting and leaving their seats likely caused the sweat. When some students continued despite her efforts, she rested her forehead on her hands for a few seconds before attempting to start over.

Her droopy blue eyes begged for relief as the students treated her classroom like a street corner or a playground. Two boys wrestled with each other in the middle of the classroom and she yelled in a hoarse voice for them to stop. Only after one of the boys yelled "Mercy," did the other one let him out of the playful choke hold. On the other side of the classroom, one boy held his pencil in between his hands as another boy attempted to break the pencil with one of his own. I found out later the game was called Pencil Pop. A few other dudes placed single dollar bills on the floor and flipped coins in a game that we sometimes played in Dearborn called Get Like Me. The player who flipped the coin second, had to match sides with the player who flipped first in order to win. I also discovered that playing Get Like Me was a way for students to gamble without using playing cards or dice, which were usually confiscated by teachers or the assistant principal. In the back of the class, three boys and one female student stood in a circle and rapped while one of the students pounded his fist on top of a desk to make a beat.

"I represent the Hunneds/ where hustlas get paid/ say the wrong thang and you might get played/ I stay fresh to def with the baby blue Js/ Baby look good see I might call her name/Chi-Town player, gotta a lot of game/I touched her one time now she gotta a lot of fame." "Ohhhh!" Each person in the circle gave the boy who rapped five who smiled with confidence. All of sudden, his smile disappeared. The boy took off his hat and sat down. The others in the group also found their seats. I turned towards the front of the class and saw a hard-looking man with a glistening baldhead and goatee standing in the doorway.

Immediately, the entire room fell silent. A nametag that read *Mr. Franks: assistant principal* was pinned on the left side of his blue suit jacket. He held a clipboard in his left hand and a pen in his right. He surveyed each of the 25 students and pointed at balled up pieces of paper as he walked through the isles in the class. The student who was nearest to the paper picked it up and put it in the trash. Mr. Franks wrote a few words on the clipboard and walked with a slow stride out of the class without ever saying a word.

Ms. Foster gained a bit of control over her class. She assigned books to each student and told us to write our names and the school year on the front page. I opened the book, which had a partially torn cover, and read the names and school years of the students who used the book before me. Curtis Williams 1979-80; Crystal Lewis 1980-81; Antonio Hill 1981-82; LaKesha Patterson 1982-83; Rasheeda McNeal 1983-84; Kym Tate 1984-85; Drakus Montgomery 1985-86; Bernard Troup 1986-87; and Raheem Muhammad 1987-88. I glanced at the publisher's page and saw a phone number, four games of tic tac toe, and a distorted drawing of an old woman with a cigarette in her mouth. The words "Ms. Foster has dragon breath," were scribbled above the drawing. On the lower right hand side of the page, "South Side 4 Life Hoe" was written in black ink. Ms. Foster instructed the class to open the books to page 18. But minutes after she began to teach about the Persian War, the school bell rang and first period was over.

It took me more than 20 minutes to locate my second period class. Whispers could be heard in room 334 as the student wrote down 15 key words that were on the chalkboard. "Dr. Hooks: Freshman Literature 10:00-10:55 a.m." was written above the words. Dr. Hooks wore a long Dashiki and had a Kenta cloth scarf tied around her dreads. She spoke with an easy tone that was authoritative without being overbearing. I hurried through the first isle and sat behind a desk that was located in the back of the classroom. I opened my notebook and realized that I didn't have a pen or pencil.

"Starting late is one thing, but being unprepared will ensure that you are irrelevant in a world that already sees you as such," the teacher pronounced before walking to my desk and handing me a sharpened pencil.

"Everyone stop writing for a second and look around. Some of you who don't know each other today will become best friends over the next four years. Some of you will disagree on things. Some of you will succeed in your studies, while others won't put forth the effort. During the next four years, the decisions that you make will determine what you will be when it is time for you to pay bills. In four years, you will learn how to be star students, star athletes, professionals and leaders. Or, you will take the first step towards the wrong path. Believe it or not, this is where your life begins.

I see it every four years. You're going to use these years to cut class and hang out, or you will take this opportunity to learn. Using the words that are on the chalk board, I want you all to write a two page essay on where you will be four years from today."

We all exhaled when the class period ended. Most of the students walked with their heads held low. We knew that it was going to be a long semester in freshman literature.

Two periods went by before I recognized a couple of familiar faces. Larry and Peanut were walking on the second floor when I spotted them.

"Whasup, Larry," I shouted as they approached.

"You tell me. How are your classes?" Larry asked.

"They're alright. I have this one teacher who is lost like hell. She probably won't make it through the year. And this other teacher with dreads, she's not cutting any slack."

"Oh, you're talking about Dr. Hooks. I heard about how she'll give you six F's for missing one assignment. She's real thorough with hers."

"I figured that much."

"But man. Do you see these chicks? I'm about to hop on a few real quick," Peanut said as he turned his head to look at a girl whose blue jean skirt stopped at the top of her thighs.

"Yeah, this ain't eighth grade no more. We're in another league. Y'all see Meathead yet?"

"Naw, Meathead ain't hanging around us no more. He's hanging with his older cousin Derrick who is in the 12th grade. It looks like he's trying to get his name out there, so he's following behind the juniors and seniors."

"Oh, it's not like that is it Joe? I guess it's just us then. I'll catch y'all after school."

Peanut, Larry and I hung tight for our first days at Dunbar. Meathead would hang during the rare times his cousin wasn't around, but we got used to seeing him follow behind the upper-classmen. We really weren't in the mix, but we quickly found out who the important people were at Dunbar.

DeAndre Dye was the most popular male student. An All-State point guard in his senior year, DeAndre had offers to play ball at several Division I colleges. He had so much pull that the teachers and administrators rarely wrote him up for cutting class. The word was that he only showed up for class during test days. The P.E. coaches allowed him to spend each class period in the gym so that he could play ball. When the coaches thought the gig was becoming routine, DeAndre would hang out at Dunbar Park with the dealers who attended school only to sell weed. If someone had told me that he owned the school, I probably would have guessed that he was the great grandson of Paul Dunbar himself.

His gear was also on another level. DeAndre always sported the best fitted caps, polo shirts, jerseys, Starter jackets and shoes. Peanut said the neighborhood dealers would take DeAndre around to different playgrounds in the city and put money on one-on-one games to 15. They would bet hundreds of dollars on DeAndre to win. A major dealer from the Robert Taylor Homes once won $5,000 from a dealer in Cabrini Green after DeAndre beat a prized Michigan State recruit by a score of 15 to 3 at Lakefront Park. Peanut claimed that the dealers paid a hype to shovel 3-feet of snow off of one half of the court before the game. He also said that DeAndre played shirtless when the temperature was just below 30 degrees. The dealer who bet on DeAndre cashed in big, but he only gave DeAndre $150 for the win. Peanut said that he usually made up for the slight in pay by playing at least 10 one-on-one games per week during the off-season. The money meant he could buy new clothes and have just about every girl in the school on his tip.

However, there was one girl at Dunbar who was out of De-Andre's reach. Her name was Imani Grier. At 5-foot-5 and around 130 pounds, the 17-year-old junior had every boy in the school plotting to figure out what it would take to get close to her. Some boys would giver her flowers, slip notes in her locker, or even offer to buy her new shoes when she ignored their pickup lines. Even the star athletes and pretty boys didn't have enough clout to get at Imani. She only went out with older dealers who wore thick gold chains and drove expensive rides. A couple of high level dudes would usually pick her up after school. The most frequent was a guy named Troy. Troy, who looked to be in his early 20s, arrived at the school every-day around 3:45 p.m. in a red Audi 5000 with gold trim. Imani would sashay to his car while her girlfriends paused to watch her open the passenger side door. Troy would usually have a car phone to his ear as Imani leaned over to kiss him. He seemed to be unmoved by her kisses, and his coolness was further validated by her being at his side.

After the lunch period ended, Larry, Peanut and I stared as Imani walked by with her shoulder-length hair, smooth brown skin and hazel colored eyes. She was classy and made a point to never wear the same outfit twice. Some days she would come to school dressed like a business professional. She would wear black high heels, a white buttoned-down shirt, black stockings and a tight black skirt that hugged her hips and displayed her curves. But she could switch styles by wearing a cut-up graffiti-painted T-shirt over a sports bra and cut-up jeans that made her resemble a lost member of Salt-N-Pepa. She was exclusive and everyone in that school knew it.

Whenever Blue and I got together to hang out, I would brag to him about all of the older girls that he was missing out on by not going to school. If he wasn't in the courtyard selling, he was likely chilling in this vacant apartment in Dearborn. A single mother who moved and handed the apartment over to her brother was the first occupant that I knew of. Her brother later lost the apartment after causing a small kitchen fire while free-basing. The CHA never attempted to restore or move anyone else in, so Blue took the apartment and made it his chill spot. It was a place where he could go to lay low and sometimes stash his product.

The floor of the vacant apartment was scattered with old newspapers. A black wall in the kitchen was evidence of the fire that occurred some years ago. Busted windows provided little protections from the cold winds that blew in from the outside. Two plastic buckets, which served as seats and a small card table were in the center of the apartment. Blue used an extension cord that ran from a neighbor's apartment to plug up his heater and lamp.

During the second week of school, I stopped by the spot on my way home to kick it with Blue.

"So you snatched any of those broads yet?" Blue asked before stuffing his mouth with Lemon Heads candy.

"Naw, those chicks are choosing on those older cats now. But I'm gonna have all their eyes when I step in there with those 23s in a couple of months," I said as Blue smirked.

"Oh, so you gonna get 'em for sure this year huh?"

"No doubt. I've been saving all summer for 'em. They come out in February. You'll see me when I step fresh in them."

"You know I got to get 'em too Joe. Matter of fact, I can get the money from that boy Fat Nate. I gave him some work this summer. Didn't charge him nothing. Just told him to pay me on the back end. It's been five months and he ain't gave me a dime. He moved to Robert Taylor and I ended up paying for all of it. He still at Dunbar right?"

Blue, knowing the answer to his own question, squinted as he thought hard about his dilemma with Fat Nate. He couldn't hide his spite. Whenever Blue became worried, he wasn't satisfied until he found a way to handle whatever was bothering him. Fat Nate had become a problem for Blue and money was hardly the issue. He put trust in Fat Nate and did not receive the proper level of repsect in return. In another place, it was probably considered petty. But in our world, it was an insult to be taken advantage of in any form.

I decided to let Blue cool down and chill alone. Besides,

Dearborn was not the place to be when the day gave way to darkness. I gave Blue five and headed home before the fights and police sirens made their presence known.

While walking out of Dearborn, I saw the tall skinny man whom Blue had pushed to the ground and spit on during the summer. He was surrounded by hypes who were all talking over each other and laughing. As I walked by the men, someone hollered from a distance, "You know you a fool for that one C-Roy!" The tall man turned and responded to the person by saying, "That's Mr. Calvin to you Earl." At that moment, all of the loud talking ceased. Everything around me became silent. The background of the Dearborn projects disappeared. Nothing else existed. The only thing that I could see was that tall man laughing. It was really him. It was the man my mom had told me so much about. It was C-Roy.

I stared at the man for a minute and a half to carve out his facial features under the glare of street lights. His eyes were sharp and glassy, and his skin was oily and coarse. Although his two front teeth were missing, he didn't hesitate to smile from ear to ear. He looked like a man who was satisfied with just being.

I walked closer to C-Roy as he continued to talk to the other hypes. I touched his shoulder. "Hey, uh what do they call you?" I asked as his smile faded. For several seconds, he looked at me from head to toe. He took a sip of what was in his brown paper bag and said, "Who wanna know?"

I looked around and noticed the other hypes staring at me. "I.. I heard someone call you C-Roy," I said while turning my head towards the hypes and then glancing back at the tall man.

"Oh yeah. Well who did you hear that from?" the tall man shouted.

"He probably heard it from yo momma," another said as the other hypes laughed.

"Do you know a lady named Tina Hall?" I asked the tall man as he mumbled the name through his lips.

"What's your name?"

"Minus."

The man dropped his head and stepped away from the other hypes. He walked toward me and his eyes filled with regret. He took a hard look at me and then stared at the ground as if it hurt to make eye contact. His mouth moved, but no words came out. The confidence that he displayed earlier was gone. C-Roy lifted his head and seemed to have gathered himself long enough to speak.

"Hey C-Roy, let's go get some good. They got some of that knock-out around the corner," a hype shouted in the distance as he and the other hypes around him began to walk in the direction of the Dearborn courtyard. C-Roy's mind found an escape and he took two steps backwards and said, "Ah, I gotta go. Tell Tina hi."

The evening sun set behind the Dearborn projects as I stood near the entrance with my hands in my pockets. Unable to move, I watched as C-Roy walked away and disappeared behind a project building with the other hypes. My emotions were unaffected. Anger did not touch me. I allowed myself to remain confused because I knew that it would hurt to even try to understand.

CHAPTER 5

The world doesn't care about where you're from.- Tina Hall

Once the bell rang on Friday afternoon, the students at Dunbar ran out of the building as if the halls were filled with fire and smoke. It was the beginning of the weekend and the day that trouble could arrive unannounced.

It was the one day out of the school week when watching your back was as important as breathing. On Fridays, I only took a notebook to school. My book bag remained at home as a safety measure. If I had to fight, I didn't want the weight of books to hold me down when I swung my fists. I walked slowly and observed everyone around me in order to make sure that no one was getting too close. That tactic was useful and allowed me to make it home without being sucker punched or sneaked.

The first day that Blue stepped on a high school campus occurred on a Friday afternoon in late October. Shortly after the bell rang, I spotted Blue outside as I made my way through the double doors at the school's main entrance. He leaned on a wall with his arms folded. As the school buses began to fill, Blue stood up straight, wrapped a white bandana around the knuckles of his right hand and ran towards a crowd of students. He slowed his pace once he made his way to the center of the crowd. Fat Nate was standing beside a girl when Blue rushed him and punched him in the face. The girl dropped her books and moved to the side. Fat Nate doubled over after Blue kneed him in the stomach and slammed him into the school bus. A crowd ran towards the fight and they both became less visible from where I was standing. The students began chanting, "FIGHT! FIGHT! FIGHT! FIGHT!" But, when I finally got close enough to view the fight, it was over.

Fat Nate stood up as his eyes began to swell and blood dripped from his nose. Blue ran away and the crowd dispersed when the school's security guards rushed toward the cluster of students. One of the security guards chased after Blue, but he gave up after realizing that Blue was too fast for his middle-aged legs. Fat Nate gathered his belongings while most of the students looked on. He made eye contact with me and stared. I paid his stare no mind. I figured he was just messed up from the ass kicking he had just received.

Once I arrived at home that evening, I picked up my grand-father's horn and played. During my improvisation, my mom walked into my room and held a card in her right hand.

"What is this Minus?" My mom asked.

"It looks like a business card."

"Darn right it's a business card. I was in your room earlier looking for batteries and I noticed this on the floor. I called the number and had a long conversation with Mr. Peterson." my mom said.

"Why?" I asked and continued to play.

"What do you mean why? And stop playing that darn horn! This man told me that he gave you his card this summer so that you could see about going to New Trier High School to play in the jazz band. He said he liked the way you played the horn and was going to try to get you into the music program."

"He's talking just to talk. That man is not gonna do anything for me. And I'm not going to school with a bunch of uptight snobs."

"Honey, you can't worry about them. You gotta do this for yourself. There's a lot of stuff going on in that school you're at. Don't think that I don't hear about what those kids are doing up there. You need to be at a school where you don't have so many distractions from your work."

"You're right."

I agreed with my mom only to get her to stop talking. I assumed she would forget about it if I didn't make a fuss. Whenever I tried to resist what she wanted, she pushed harder to make me see things her way. I learned that agreeing was the only thing that would shorten her argument. Soon enough, she walked out of my room and I forgot about the entire issue. I figured it was over, but my mother woke me up the next morning before sunrise and told me to get dressed and to bring my grandfather's horn.

We caught the bus to my grandmother's home at six o'clock that morning. She allowed my mom to borrow her old station wagon and we drove 30 minutes north to Winnetka. I noticed a change in scenery the farther we drove north. Abandoned buildings, miles of projects and the littered streets of the South Side were replaced with manicured lawns, three-story homes and expensive cars in the surrounding neighborhoods near

Winnetka. My mom turned into the parking lot of a school that resembled a college campus I saw in a TV commercial. The grass was cut neatly and the trees and bushes were edged into perfect round shapes. There was a small garden that held colorful flowers that was next to a red picnic table which looked unused. As we made our way to the entrance, I saw a sign that read, "New Trier High School." The South Side of Chicago and Winnetka were two different worlds that existed in the same state.

After we entered the school building, an older woman stopped us and asked if we needed help. My mom told the woman that I was there for an audition with the jazz band and the woman gave us directions to the band studio's waiting room. Fifteen students and their parents were in the room. The students held tubas, saxophones, trombones, flutes, clarinets and trumpets. A few of the students moved nervously as they sat in their seats. They appeared to be worried about what fate might hold for them if they made even half of a mistake during the audition. The sweat that trickled down their anxious faces caused me to wonder if they were auditioning for a chance at life.

Once my mother and I sat down, I noticed that I was the only black student in the entire room. Besides the time my grandfather took me to a White Sox game for my seventh birthday, I had had very little exposure to people of different ethnic backgrounds. There was a brief silence in the room after my mom and I took our seats. While some parents weren't as obvious, a few stared at us without hesitation. One parent broke the silence by mentioning how much she liked my trumpet and then asked where we stayed. "Do you live in Winnetka, or are you going to get bused from your neighborhood?" I'm sure that she wanted to make sure that our presence at her child's school and neighborhood was only a visit.

Some of the parents attempted to be more genuine, but it was impossible for a real conversation to occur with padded remarks such as, "I know you're going to make your momma proud by playing that horn," or "If you don't play well this time, I hear that you can always come back next year and try out." The entire room pretended to ignore the obvious, so I returned the favor by ignoring everyone in the room until they called me in to audition.

An hour after we arrived, a woman called my name and escorted me into the music room. Oil paintings of older men and women holding instruments hung on the walls. A shiny black piano was in the corner next to a large wooden bookshelf that held what looked like over 100 books. Two men and a woman sat behind a table with pens in their hands and sheets of paper scattered on the table. One of the men behind the table was Mr. Peterson.

"I'm Rose Bailey, this is George Wyche, and I'm sure you're already familiar with Thomas Peterson. We have several other students who are waiting to audition so we're going to get started by asking a few questions.

Mr. Hall, what do you hope to accomplish by attending this school and becoming a member of the jazz band?" The woman asked while looking at my middle school transcript.

"I just want to play a little music, that's it."

"How long have you played the trumpet?"

"Ahh, I'm guessing for about five years."

"Are you comfortable with reading music?"

"I don't really read music like that. I kind of play what I feel."

"Have you played in the school's band or taken any

formal music classes?" Mr. Wyche interrupted.

"I mean, I used to watch my grandfather play. That's about it. And I listen to Miles Davis every now and then."

Ms. Bailey and Mr. Wyche both looked at Mr. Peterson who moved uneasily in his seat. Mr. Peterson cleared his throat and said, "OK Minus, there will be no further questions. Is there a selection that you wish to play." I played my favorite Miles Davis song and they all listened and took notes. About 30 seconds into the song, Ms. Bailey interrupted and said, "Thank you. We have enough."

"That was a waste of time," I told my mom as we drove back to my grandmother's home.

"What do you mean it was a waste a time?" my mom fired back.

"They probably always picked one student from the South Side to audition for their school's jazz band. They wanted to make it seem like they were giving me a fair chance. All of it was just a big front."

"Even if it was just a front, how many boys from the South Side got a chance to do what you just did? How many of your friends at Dunbar got a chance to see something different? I didn't see Larry, Meatboy, or Blue in there today. So don't come telling me it was a waste of time. Because as far as I'm concerned, you still have a chance to be one step ahead of where you were yesterday."

"I don't care about that. I would rather go to school on the South Side with real people instead of being around folks who think they're better than us."

"Minus, you're the only one who can think that someone is better than you. The world doesn't care about where you're from. All that matters is what you know."

My mom's argument did little to convince me. I knew that those people did not want me in their school. It was a game to them and I was just their pawn. But I could not blame my mom for thinking the way that she did. She was just a victim of Mr. Peterson's version of fool's gold.

CHAPTER 6

I had just entered a supreme class.- Minus Hall

My excitement was intensified by the arrival of the New Year. It was 1989 and the countdown to the release date of the new 23s had begun. During the weeks approaching the February release, I scratched off days on my calendar in anticipation. I hung posters, basketball cards, and banners of MJ on the walls of my room. I even bought the video *Come Fly With Me* in order to capture the entire experience.

The one-hour video showed all of MJ's basketball highlights as he told his life story. In the video, he revealed that he got cut from his high school's basketball team. The greatest person to ever pick up a basketball was once told that he wasn't good enough to play. That made having the shoes even more important. It showed that failure was a human trait, but being satisfied with it was unacceptable. MJ proved that anything could be overcome if hard work was applied. In MJ, I no longer saw a man that could dunk a basketball. I saw a man who was normal, until he decided to jump. When he jumped, failure was beneath him. He was proof that there was really a way out.

Every day I put that tape in my mother's VCR and watched it until she demanded that I turn it off and do homework or play the horn. She didn't understand how I could watch the same video over and over. But it was not a rerun to me. Every time I watched *Come Fly With Me*, I was seeing it for the first time.

The night before the 23s were released, I laid in the dark and thought about finally owning the shoes. This time, there was nothing in my way. I didn't have to hope and wait for someone to get them for me. The money that I saved over the summer spoke for me. I held the money tightly in my right hand the entire night.

I managed to fall asleep for two hours before my alarm clock rang at 6:35 a.m. I showered, brushed my teeth and got dressed for the big event. I ate a bowl of cereal and again watched *Come Fly With Me* before leaving my apartment at 7:15 a.m.

Most of the shoe stores on the South Side opened at 11a.m. I figured that the students at Dunbar would probably wait until after school to get the new 23s. But I had another plan. I wanted to be the first person at Dunbar with the shoes. So instead of waiting until after school, I decided to take the train to Stoney's Shoe Store & Clothing. Stoney's was located on South Bishop Street on the West Side. It was a popular spot for the folks who stayed near my grandmother's home.

Stoney's was owned by an older man name Walter Berg. Walter Berg was known around the neighborhood as a shrewd businessman who was always searching for a way to make a dollar. Before he opened Stoney's, he owned three polish sausage stands at different locations around the city. The word was that he got the idea to open Stoney's after a group of teenage boys attempted to steal money from one of his stands. Walter Berg was able to catch one of the boys by grabbing the collar of his jacket. The boy stopped immediately and begged Walter Berg not to stretch his $100 Starter jacket. Walter Berg agreed to let the boy go if he showed him where he bought his jacket. Soon after, Walter Berg sold all three of his polish sausage stands and opened a small store that sold the latest Starter apparel, Adidas, Reeboks, Nikes, and 23s. He found there was a greater demand in the neighborhood for athletic gear than polish sausages.

I arrived at Stoney's shortly after 8 a.m. The store opened two hours earlier than most of the shoe stores in the city. A large white banner with red letters hung above the entrance to the store. The sign read, "New Air Jordans For Sale Today!" I opened the door and at least 15 customers were already in the store. I tapped one guy on the shoulder and asked him where the line ended. He looked down at my shoes and said, "You're the last one with a spot. I suggest you hold on to it."

Those nearest to the cash register often glanced at their watches and the clock as the sales reps hustled back and forth to fill their orders. While the sales reps scrambled, I surveyed every person inside of the store to see if anyone from Dunbar was there. I smiled inside after seeing so many unfamiliar faces that morning.

Twenty minutes after I arrived, the line was at a standstill. The customers became more hostile as the slow service worsened.

"I don't have all day!"

"This is ridiculous!"

"Are y'all making the 23s?"

"You all need more workers in this dump!"

Customers continued to fuss as the sales reps ran to the

storage room to retrieve the 23s from a location guarded by four police officers.

"They're taking special precautions this year," the customer who stood in front of me observed.

"I see. Why are so many police up here? Shouldn't they be outside directing traffic or something?" I asked.

"This is all the traffic they need. Rush hour on the Dan Ryan won't be as busy as the shoe stores today. Last year, a riot almost broke out here. People spent the night outside in the snow just to be the first ones to get inside. When the doors opened at 8 a.m., they rushed the door and WrestleMania damn near broke out. People were pushing and shoving like they were giving away million dollar bills. The fire department showed up and made everybody leave. I'm not even buying shoes today. I'm just here to see what's gonna happen next."

A short pudgy sales rep in his late `20s looked in my direction and said, "What size, cat?"

"Size 11" I replied.

"Let me get an 11 out of the back, Lisa," the rep screamed.

"We're out of 11," the girl yelled from the storage room.

"How can you all be out of size 11? You knew that everybody was gonna come here early. It's not even 9 o'clock yet. What type of backwards operation are you all running?"

The sales rep could sense my anger and walked to the back to see if he could find my shoe size. Time was elapsing. I was already late for my first period class and I still did not have the 23s to show for it. I spent the entire summer saving for this moment and saw it going down the drain. I didn't just want those shoes. At that point, I needed them.

The sales rep returned with a shoe box in his right hand. He approached me and then opened the box. Inside were the red, black and white shoes that bore the Jumpman emblem across the tongue. Two black and red rubber straps sprung from the sides, four inches above the air-bubbled shoe soles. The white net and leather side gave the shoes style. If there was anything that could come close to the Holy Grail, it was right before me in a cardboard shoebox.

"All we have is size 11 ½," the sales rep said.

"Damn, you sure you all don't have size 11?" I asked.

"Naw cat. That's it. Double up on socks and you'll be alright. You wanna try`em on?"

I took off my L.A. Gears and slid the 23s on my feet. The shoes were light weight and well-cushioned inside. I pulled the tongue so the Jumpman symbol was more visible. I rubbed my fingers across the leather side to feel the toughness of the material. After walking a few feet and doing five toe lifts to test out the stability, I did two jumping jacks.

"Yo, cat! Are you about to run a basketball marathon? You testing the shoes like you just signed a contract with the Bulls or somethin'. Are you buying the shoes or what? Cause if not, I got people in line who are waiting to get those son." the sales rep said while pointing at five customers who walked into the store after I did.

I looked at the 23s and glanced down at my own shoes. Playing those L.A. Gears for another day was not an option. I figured that no one would notice that my shoes were a half size too big, so I decided to purchase them. I placed $110 on the cashier's counter and once Walter Berg handed me a receipt, it was official.

I walked out of the store with a semi-George Jefferson strut and placed my old shoes on the sidewalk next to a homeless man who was asleep. My new 23s were the only shoes that I would need to wear. The red, white and black shoes matched the red extra large hooded sweat shirt that hung over my 5-7, 170 pound frame. My box hair cut was still fresh two days after Hassan cut it. And the black jeans set my outfit off. I had just entered a supreme class. I was now a 23 owner.

Chapter 7

Your eyes say that you're suspicious.- Meta Sinclair

I arrived at Dunbar as the students were leaving their first period classes. After walking through the entrance of the school building, the hallway felt like a red carpet and I was the star arriving at my own premiere. My first semester at Dunbar lacked excitement and I was still an unknown freshmen. But that day, I owned something that no one else in the school had in their possession. That one thing changed my life.

My new 23s captivated nearly everyone in the school. I walked through the hallways and noticed students whispering and pointing at my shoes while looking on in awe. Even DeAndre Dye and his teammates stopped to stare. It was probably the first time that anyone overshadowed DeAndre when it came to being fresh to def at Dunbar. He admitted defeat by saying, "Hey, Lil Joe. I like those." I replied, "Thanks" and kept walking without ever breaking stride.

Before the start of third period, Meathead hung by my locker for the first time that school year. He gave me five and began to talk.

"Minus, what's up man?"

"Nothing much. I'm chilling, Meat," I replied.

"Man, those 23s are looking nice. You probably dropped a lot for 'em huh?"

"Yeah, they cost a pretty penny."

"I bet all of the chicks are trying to get at you now. What class are you headed to next?"

I didn't have a problem with Meathead showing my shoes love, but he followed me around the school the entire day as if he was my personal assistant. Considering that we had not hung around each other since entering high school, I figured that he was only around to stand next to the guy with the new 23s. But I forgave him for his insincerity. We grew up together so I allowed him to feel what it was like to walk next to my shoes.

My 23s fascinated most of the students, but there were a few who envied me. They wouldn't say a word, but I could feel the hate by the way they squinted. It hurt them to see the 23s on my feet. I understood that they wanted what I owned. So I stared back with a slight smile to show my amusement.

After lunch, I hung around my locker with Meathead, Larry and Peanut. Other guys who were friends of Larry and Meathead hung around also. My 23s were catching a lot of eyes and they probably thought that the attention would shift towards them by standing next to me. So they all struck up a phony conversation about MJ to make it all relevant.

"Hey, man, did y'all see how MJ dropped 45 points on Cleveland the other day?" one of Meathead's friends asked.

"Yeah I saw that game. The man can't be stopped," Larry answered.

"Man, me and my little brother was watching this movie

called *The Clonus Horror* the other day. And I was thinking, they should clone MJ so that he could be the only person on the team. If they did that, the Bulls would never lose," Meathead said.

"Meathead, how stupid do you sound? He's only 6-foot-6. If they had five MJs on the team, who's gonna play center?" Peanut asked.

"He's gonna play center, point guard, shooting guard, small forward and power forward. And he's gonna come off the bench. I'm telling you now, I'll pay with my life to see that," Meathead said as if he truly believed his own ridiculous remarks.

Laughs would usually follow such a dense statement, but everyone standing in the group became quiet and turned their heads to the right. I looked to my right and saw Imani and a group of girls walking towards us. Her hair was curled and glowed as if she'd just stepped out of the shower. She wore a short black leather jacket, a green cashmere turtleneck, black tights, and black high heels.

If one person could outshine MJ himself, it was Imani. But even she could not ignore the power of the 23 brand. In what seemed like slow motion, she looked past everyone who stood beside me. She looked down at my shoes, we made eye contact and she said, "What's up?" In an attempt to remain extra cool, I nodded in response. I suddenly had the biggest balls in the entire school.

All of the boys who were around me nudged my shoulder and gave me five. They then pressed me with their own comments about the matter.

"Man, she's choosing on you!"

"Boy you better hop on that quick."

"If I had that, I know what I'd do."

"Minus ain't gonna do nothing with that."

"Let her come at me, she'd get it fast." I was on top of the world. Imani Grier spoke to me as if we had had previous conversations. And she wasn't the type of girl who just spoke to anyone. She made sure that she didn't waste her breath on people that were less important than her. For her to speak to me was big, and all of my boys knew it.

Imani speaking to me was only the beginning. After fifth period, a sophomore named Meta Sinclair approached me while I was putting my folder in my locker. Meta was well-known because she hung around Imani. We had never spoken before, so I figured she was at my locker to relay a message from Imani. But Meta's visit was more than a message delivery.

"What's up, Minus?" she asked.

"Nothing," I replied a bit puzzled about how she knew my name.

"Where did you get those 23s from?"

"I got them from this spot on the West Side called Stoney's."

"Those are fresh. My brother said he's gonna get some this weekend."

"That's cool."

"Don't you stay by West 26th Street?"

"Yeah, um. A little bit."

"You know my aunt stays down the street from you. I thought I saw you walking over there with a horn in your hand one day."

"Probably so. Where you stay?"

"By Metcalf Park. It's not that far if you take the CTA."

"I know. That's over there near the Robert Taylor

Homes."

"If you want, you can meet me after school and we can go to my house and listen to some music or something. My mother works late tonight. She won't be home until after midnight."

"Is your brother gonna be there?"

"Naw. He's 26 and has his own place. I have a younger brother too, but he's staying at my aunt's house tonight."

"Word. I'll meet you right here after school then."

"OK."

I thought about Meta during the entire sixth period. Of all the days, I wondered why Meta picked that day to come on to me. Meta was an average looking girl. She was a 5-foot-4 red bone whose hair stopped just below her ear, and a few pimples dotted her face. Her butt was probably her most attractive feature. Her body could turn a few heads, but she wasn't nearly as fine as Imani. Meta seemed to admire Imani's beauty along with everyone else at Dunbar. And just like a new pair of 23s, girls either admired Imani or envied her. Meta looked nice enough to hang with Imani without overshadowing her. She was like the Secretary of Treasury to the President. You knew she existed, but you only noticed her when the President was around.

Meta and I met outside of Dunbar after school. We caught the CTA instead of the school bus to keep my visit to her home discreet. She lived in a duplex near Metcalfe Park that was a few blocks away from the Robert Taylor Homes.

Meta unlocked the burglar bar screen door and I walked into her home. A large cabinet filled with framed pictures of Meta and her family members was the first thing in sight when she opened the front door. There were several baby pictures of her and one that showed her as a toothless little girl in a private school uniform. Another picture showed her standing with an older man flashing a wad of money in his right hand. In the picture, she wore a T-shirt that had "Daddy's Girl" air-brushed on it.

The black leather couch in the living room felt more like soft rubber. And the coffee table and lamps reminded me of something out of a Rent-A-Center commercial. But the most intriguing thing about Meta's apartment was the TV. In a living room with unassuming furniture, the TV was the centerpiece of her home. At what appeared to be close to 42 inches, the TV dwarfed everything in the apartment.

Meta plugged up her VCR and put in the movie *The Last Dragon*. With the wide screen, surround sound and dim lights, her living room had the feeling of a movie theatre. I was amazed at the super-sized visuals of watching Bruce Leroy battle Sho Nuff as they captured The Glow.

When the movie ended, Meta unplugged her VCR and turned on the stereo. She placed a cassette in the tape deck and sat down next to me on the couch.

"Minus, you know your eyes are like a tiger. They're relaxed, but at the same time focused. You try not to make it noticeable, but your eyes say that you're suspicious about a lot of things," Meta said as I chuckled.

"Why you laughing? I'm for real. I wanna know something, though. Why don't you ever speak to us when we're at school?" Meta asked.

"What do you mean?"

"I always see you hanging around that locker with those other boys who be making noises and hissing when we walk by. They act desperate and like they never saw a girl before. But you never say 'what's up' or nothing. Like you all cool and stuff. You know, most of my friends think that you're cute."

"I didn't know you were looking that close. If I had known, I probably would've said something."

"OK. So when I see you in the hall are you gonna speak now?"

"No doubt."

Meta's brother, who was a part-time DJ, left three crates of records and tapes at her home. Meta searched through the crates and played records by Slick Rick, Boogie Down Productions, and Big Daddy Kane. When Big Daddy Kane's "Ain't No Half Steppin," came on, Meta stepped up on the coffee table and began to do the Wop dance.

"Oh snap, this is my jam. Big Daddy Kane is my favorite rapper. No offense, but he's soooo fine! Do you like to dance Minus?"

"I never really got into dancing."

"I don't know why you boys always act like you all are too cool to dance."

"I don't think I'm too cool. I try to do the Bobby Brown when I'm at home, but it never comes out right. Maybe you should teach me."

"Are you willing to follow my instructions?"

"I'll follow your instructions, if we can start with slow dancing."

Meta took off the Big Daddy Kane record and rummaged through the crate for R & B music. She picked up albums by Anita Baker, Sade, New Edition and Luther Vandross. Meta chose to play Sade.

Meta asked me to stand as she grabbed my right hand and placed it on her hip. She then took my left hand and began to move side to side.

"I was really joking. I only thought that people slow danced in the movies and on TV," I told Meta as we began our slow dance.

"Come on Minus, you're from the 'hood, but you're not that hood."

"I'm not going to argue with that because sophomores know everything, right? But on the real, how did you learn how to slow dance?"

"I went to a private elementary school from kindergarten until the sixth grade. The teachers and parents always made this big fuss about the sixth graders attending the annual debutante ball. So I was forced to participate in these boring dance classes for nearly two months straight."

"Guess those lessons came in handy, huh?"

"Yup, all so that I can teach you a thing or two. Do you like Sade?"

"I never bought any of her tapes, but I like her sound," I said.

"I love Sade. I just get so relaxed when I hear her. I listen to her album every night before I go to sleep."

I pulled Meta closer as she rested her head on my left shoulder and closed her eyes. Sade's voice and the background sax were the only sounds resonating in the apartment. She grabbed my hand tighter and lifted her head from my shoulder. Our eyes connected and then we kissed. Meta stopped kissing me and asked, "Are you gonna take those off?" I looked down at my 23s and looked back at her. I untied them slowly and hated that I would have to take them off in her apartment. Thoughts of someone breaking into her apartment and taking my 23s entered my mind as I took off my right shoe. I could have gotten with Meta anytime, but those 23s were too important to lay them on the floor at her house. As soon as my left shoe was off, those thoughts were erased as Meta kissed me again.

"I'm about to go home and get some sleep. First period is kinda hard on the eyes if you know what I mean." I whispered in Meta's ear an hour later. She turned and fiddled through a box on her dresser before grabbing my left wrist. With a black ink pen in between her fingers, she wrote in the palm of my hand.

"This is my number Minus. Are you gonna be able to put it to use sometime?"

"Yeah, I can make that happen."

She handed me the pen when she finished and I wrote my phone number on the palm of her right hand. As I slid into my shoes, I noticed that a small dirt spot was on the side of my 23s. I got a napkin out of Meta's kitchen and wiped the spot off before leaving her apartment.

"You really love those shoes. I see that you can't stand to get 'em dirty," she said as I put on my sweatshirt.

"I think you know about the deal with these shoes. What time does the next bus come?"

"The next bus should be pulling up at the stop in about five minutes. Here, I'll walk you to the door."

I walked out of Meta's apartment 10 minutes after eleven o'clock. I knew my mother would be angry with me coming home late, but it didn't matter. I was on a natural high and there was nothing she could say or do to bring me down. I didn't care about the tongue lashing that she would give me or the potential grounding. The day was perfect and any repercussion was well worth it. My 23s earned me great returns on my $110 investment. DeAndre Dye showed respect by acknowledging my sneaks; Meathead hung around like a flunky; Imani's eyes were on me; and I got with a chick who hadn't spoken to me before that day.

A few hypes and dealers were outside walking around as I sat down at the edge of the sidewalk near the bus stop. While sitting down with my hood over my head, I thought about new possibilities. I spent the evening with Meta, but Imani was the only girl I could think about. Getting with Meta gave me the confidence to finally approach Imani. If I had enough pull to get with a sophomore like Meta, I could have probably mustered up a little more game to get with Imani. She spoke to me in the hallway, so she must have wanted to kick it with me. All I needed to do was strike up a conversation with Imani, get her phone number and find a way to hook up with her outside of school.

The world was in my hands. I was already the first guy in school with the new 23s, and I suddenly felt as if I could be the first guy to pull Imani. I would be the most popular freshman in school without a doubt. DeAndre Dye would beg me to hang with him and his boys. I would have flunkies like Meathead and his boys running behind me so that they could be known as the dudes who stood next to my locker. Every girl would be jealous and intrigued because I was involved with the best-looking chick in school. For the next four years, I would have my pick of any girl I wanted. And all of the haters would have more ammunition to dislike the freshman who had the 23s and the chicks on his tip. I was about to become one of the most popular students at Dunbar High. It was only a matter of time.

After 10 minutes of pondering on what could be, I stood up and looked down the street to my left to see if the bus was arriving. I glanced at my digital watch and it read 11:17p.m. I bent over to wipe off my left shoe. On my way back up, someone snuck behind me and shoved me in the back. I stumbled forward and ran about four steps before I was grabbed by the collar and slammed onto the pavement. I turned around and saw two dudes wearing skull caps and hooded coats. Black bandanas covered their nose and mouth, but their merciless eyes were in plain view. I jumped up from the pavement and hit one of the dudes in the face. Soon after my punch landed, the other guy grabbed me from behind and put a chokehold around my neck.

"Man, hit him again. This little sucka think we playin," the dude who had me in the chokehold said.

"Forget that. Take `em. I got `em by the neck. He ain't goin' no where!"

The guy I hit began punching me in the stomach as the other one used his forearm to squeeze my neck tighter. I began gasping for air and coughing. Instinctively, I rammed my elbow to the right side of the dude who held my neck. He was stunned by the blow and released my neck from the grip. He folded over and covered his ribs. I punched him in the same side again before the other guy grabbed me and threw me back on the pavement. The guy who I punched in the side pulled out a switchblade. He began to swing the blade towards my stomach, but the other guy grabbed his arm.

"Don't worry about that. This punk ain't nothing."

They both kicked and stomped on me as I covered my face while on the ground. My arms were no match for their blows. With my face pressed against the pavement, I was kicked for one final time before they both ran away. I put my hands on my nose and saw blood as I looked down at my index finger. The bitter taste of blood filled my mouth as I spit a wad of it out on the sidewalk. I could barely open my right eye, so I glanced out of my left eye and looked down. I noticed that I only had socks on my feet.

CHAPTER 8

Where your 23s, man?-Meathead

"Talk to me."

"What's up Blue?"

"Nothing at all, Joe. Just at the crib chilling, I'm about to knock it out for the night. What's up on your end?"

"You won't guess what just happened, brah."

"Not without a clue."

"Man, I went over to this chick's house today after school…"

"Word? Did you smash?"

"Forget about that. Around 11, I left her house and went outside to catch the bus. Before I knew it, these two suckers crept up behind me. I handled it the best I could, but they got the best of me. They took the shoes."

"Your 23s?"

"Yeah, my 23s."

"Where were you at?"

"I was by Metcalfe Park."

"Man, that's over there by them Taylor boys. You know they don't play fair. I wouldn't step near that place without having something on me. Did you see their faces?"

"Naw, they had on bandanas and I was too busy swinging to get a good look."

"How long have you been home?"

"A few hours. My mom is all worried so I gotta get off this horn."

"I tell you what. You question that girl who you were with. She might have had you set up. If you think she even had a little something to do with it, you need to handle it."

"I'll see what's going on. I'm gonna talk to you tomorrow."

"Ight, Joe."

The next day, I entered Dunbar High with a gash on my lip and a large knot under my right eye. With my 23s gone, the only shoes that I owned were an old torn up pair of Kangaroos sneakers. DeAndre Dye regained his title for the freshest dressed as he strolled down the hall wearing the new 23s, a red Polo shirt, and a black Chicago Bulls Starter jacket.

Meathead stopped by my locker after third period and looked down at my sneakers. My socks were noticeable due to the hole on the right side of my Kangaroos. Meathead bent down, put his finger in the hole and asked, "Where your 23s at man?"

"You won't believe…" I began to explain before Meathead interrupted.

"Hey, man. Let me get back to you. I gotta do something real quick," Meathead said as he followed behind his cousin Derrick, who passed us in the hall. Some people spoke, but the stares were absent. No one looked on in amazement. All that seemed real the previous day disappeared from my reality. I was a regular student again.

I stood alone by my locker after leaving the cafeteria during lunch. The guys who hung near my locker the day before were not around. Imani and her crew strolled through the hallway as they did each day after lunch. Wearing a black halter top and jeans that hugged her perfect thighs, Imani led the way as her friends followed. I placed a mint in my mouth and put my hands in my pockets. I crossed my left foot over my right foot to cover up the hole on the side of my shoe. I leaned against my locker as the girls got closer. I anticipated Imani speaking again. I planned to take the moment to compliment her outfit. It was a gesture that would surely make her blush and allow me to flirt with the best looking girl in the school. As she approached, I opened my mouth, but no words came out. Imani never looked in my direction.

Meta walked alongside Imani, listening to her every word as if she was a preacher. I tried to get Meta's attention, but she continued to follow Imani. I then shouted her name. She turned and said, "What, Minus?"

"What!?" I replied. "So it's like that now?"

"No, I just have to go to class. Can we catch up later?"

Meta rushed back to Imani's side without giving me a chance to respond. I clenched my teeth and snatched my political science folder out of my locker. As I headed toward class, Peanut and Larry stood in the hall and put out their hands to give me five. But I nodded and kept walking without saying a word to either of them.

My mind wandered during fifth period. I took a seat in the back of the classroom and could hardly stay focused on the political science lesson. Meta was the only person I thought about the entire period. She had to know something about my shoes being taken. Why would she sleep with me one night and ignore me the next day? Maybe it wasn't me or the 23s that attracted Meta. She might have been attracted to the idea that she could get with someone who Imani was interested in. She probably planned the whole thing as soon as Imani looked in my direction. Meta talked me into going to her house, and she spoke as if she noticed me before that day. But it was all in her game. Or, someone could have paid her to lure me to that neighborhood. She knew that a bus would not arrive at the time that she told me. As soon as I walked outside her apartment, she could have placed the call to the boys who took my shoes at the bus stop. I chose to be with her too soon. I didn't know anything about Meta or the things that she was capable of doing.

My thoughts were interrupted once the period bell rang. After leaving the class, Larry and Peanut approached me at my locker. With a concerned look on his face, Larry asked,

"What's going on, Minus? Everything cool?"

"Naw, I'm just upset about some stuff that happened last night. Somebody got me for my 23s," I said as I slammed my locker door shut.

"Damn, that's really messed up. So that's why your eye is swollen, huh?"

"Yeah."

"Do you know who did…"

Before Larry could finish asking his question, my attention turned towards Meta as she exited her fifth period classroom alone. I called out her name and she continued to walk. I ran up to her, grabbed her arm and asked, "Did you set me up?"

"What are you talking about? Let my arm go!" Meta snapped while pulling away from my grip.

"Hell no! Somebody took my shoes after I left your house last night and I think you know who did it," I said with my finger pointing just inches from her face.

"I don't know nothing!"

"Yes you do. I should take my hand and…"

Larry pulled me away from Meta and tried his best to calm me down. Meta covered her face and ran into the girl's restroom. I jerked away from Larry and followed after Meta. I was on the verge of pulling her out of the restroom when a couple of teachers ordered me to stop. I turned and kicked the silver garbage can that was next to the water fountain. Soda cans, potato chip wrappers, and loose paper spilled from the garbage can. I stepped over the garbage and continued down the hall until I reached the front entrance of the school.

Mr. Franks saw me walking down the hall and yelled, "If you leave, don't think about coming back!" I ignored his warning and pushed the silver handles that released the locks on the metal doors. Last period did not mean a thing. I needed to get away. I knew that if I had stayed one second longer, something or someone in that school was going to get messed up.

CHAPTER 9

He's gonna be like the others before him.- Mr. Franks

On my way home from school, I watched every person on the street who wore new 23s. I studied their movements and stared into their eyes convinced that they would flinch once they saw the person they robbed the day before. If I encountered one person who looked suspicious, I was going to punch them in the face, take my shoes back and deal with whatever I would have to deal with.

But no one on the CTA or street gave me enough reason to attack. I began to look at the entire situation as something that was out of my reach. The task of finding the two suckers who jumped me would be close to impossible. Thousands of people in Chicago owned the new 23s. It would have taken me forever to size up every single person who wore those shoes. Reality hit me as I reached the steps to my apartment. I played the game and lost. It was just time to move on.

Shortly after 8:00 p.m., I was interupted from playing the horn when the phone rang.

"Hello," I answered the call.

"Can I speak to Minus?"

"This is Minus speaking. Who is this?"

"Meta."

"Oh. Hey."

"I called to tell you that I didn't have anything to do with your shoes being taken," she said adamantly.

"All I can do is take your word."

"But I think I know who might have had something to do with it."

"I'm listening."

"Well, I took the school bus home today. I sat in the front because I didn't feel like being bothered. After the bus drove away from the school, a group of boys were in the back talking loud. Now I'm not sure if any of this is true, but they were laughing about how Winky and Fat Nate took your shoes."

"Fat Nate?"

"That's what they said."

"Who is Winky?"

"He's a little older than me. He stays over there in Robert Taylor. All he does is smoke weed all day and steal from people. He went to Dunbar last year, but he dropped out."

"Damn, I'm sorry about the way I…." Before I could apologize, Meta hung up the phone. She wanted me to know that she was still angry over the way that I approached her in school. But I could not blame her for being upset — she had every right to be.

Her phone call changed my direction. Fat Nate was the type of person who would try to get over on anyone who came across his path. I thought back and remembered the hard look that he gave me after his fight with Blue. Because Blue and I were close, Fat Nate may have wanted to get back at Blue by attacking me. And the day after I was robbed, I remember seeing Fat Nate wearing the new 23s at school.

I called Blue after talking with Meta. I told him the information she gave me and he was down to help me get back at whoever took the shoes.

"Man, I'm ready to get at Fat Nate now. I don't have a problem kicking his butt again," Blue said in an excited tone.

"I'm not sure about Meta and what she's saying at this point. If she has something against Fat Nate, what better way to get back at him than by using me to do all the work? I go running after him and she gets what she wants without lifting a finger. Or she could be straight up and the people she heard this from could be lying," I said.

"Whatever man. If it's a lie, you still have to beat his ass off that lie. You gotta let people know that they just can't take shit from you. If you let one person take from you, everybody is gonna try to get a piece. And if you're known as a punk around here, you might as well be dead."

"I hear you. Well I have to get off this phone because my mom just came home from work. I'll let you know something tomorrow."

"Your call homeboy."

I thought about Blue's words while I dealt with my problems at Dunbar. Because I walked out during school hours, I was considered a truant. The school's administrators suspended me until my mom could find time to escort me to school. Once she was able to secure a day off, we both met with the assistant principal, Mr. Franks. I missed two days of school and Mr. Franks decided to give me in-school suspension for three days. But my mom wasn't satisfied with my punishment, she wanted more done.

"I'll be honest with you Mr. Franks. I don't understand what's going on with this boy. Ever since he came to this school, he's had problems staying focused. I'm wondering if there is a program that could help him to stay on track with his school work. I'm trying as hard as I can, but I can't do this by myself," my mom told Mr. Franks, while we sat in his office.

"Is there a father or an older sibling who can help out?" Mr. Franks asked.

"No. It's just me and him. And I can't keep up with everything that he does. I have to work extra hours just so that we can have electricity and food on the table."

"I'm sorry Ms. Hall, but I believe that it all starts at the home. Minus is old enough to know right from wrong and there is only so much the school system can do. We have a number of students who have disciplinary problems and we really don't have the time or resources to deal with them all. They usually become distractions to the kids who are trying to learn. If Minus can't get his act together, he's going to get kicked out of this school. And when that happens, he's going to be like the others. He will end up out in the streets where jail or the graveyard will be holding a place for him."

Mr. Franks thanked my mother for coming and opened the door to his office. My mother's problems were not a concern for Mr. Franks. To him, she was just another single mother who wanted someone else to be responsible for raising her son. But I was not lacking parental guidance or any of that other bullshit that Mr. Franks wanted to suggest without saying outright. It didn't have anything to do with her. I was going through some stuff. And in the process, I was losing control.

The administrators used in-school suspension to isolate the troubled students. I could not attend my regular classes, or eat lunch with the rest of the student body. The former football coach, Mr. Mackey, supervised 12 other students and me. We were forced to sit quietly with our desks facing the walls in a room located in the school's basement. The room had no windows and the heating system did not work in the basement. Every morning, Mr. Mackey would set up one small space heater in the center of the room. The only things that it kept warm were the spiders and bugs that crawled near it. Besides a manual hand clock that hung next to a school calendar, the white walls were completely bare. This was the school's jail and it felt as if we were being trained for the real thing.

I thought the time alone would have helped me calm down, but it only made me angrier. Fat Nate fueled my anger when I saw him on my last day of my in-school suspension. He and I bumped shoulders as I walked to the bus stop after school. He looked me up and down as I glanced at the 23s that he wore and said, "What you staring at sucker?" I squared myself directly in front of him and balled my fists. Before I could swing my right arm, the school's security guard stepped in between us. Fat Nate laughed and pointed at my shoes as he walked away from me. I stared at him until the security guard ordered me to get on the bus. At that moment, I realized what had to be done.

CHAPTER 10

I can't control what goes on out there.- Blue

Relentless February winds blew hard on the Saturday afternoon that I arrived at Blue's grandmother's apartment in Dearborn. On most occasions, I would meet Blue at the spot, or catch up with him at the courtyard. Two years had passed since the last time Blue and I met at his grandmother's apartment. I walked up the four flights of stairs in building 2971 and knocked three times on the steel door that was partly coated with fading green paint. Blue's grandmother opened the door.

"Who is that?" A female voice shouted in the background. "This Minus. Terrance little friend," Blue's grandmother shouted back. I walked into the apartment which smelled like damp carpet and cigarettes. Blue's cousin, Andrea, sat on the couch and placed a cigarette butt in a black ashtray while her four kids ran through the living room playing tag.

"Y'all stop running in this house and put your coats on! If y'all keep acting up, I ain't gonna take y'all nowhere,"

Andrea said as she stood up from the couch and put a brown wool coat over her wide body. She then walked out of the living room and gathered her kids. Blue's 9-year-old sister India walked into the living room wearing a pink coat and white gloves. Her hair was braided neatly and her brown cheeks were shining as if she had just rubbed a gob of Vaseline on her face.

"Blue's in the shower Minus," India said as she waited for her cousins to come back into the living room.

"OK. You still making A's in school," I asked.

"Yes."

"That's good. When you get out of the second grade later this year, I'm going to buy you a toy."

"Come on y'all. I'm not 'bout to be in this cold all day! We gonna walk to the store and don't ask me for nothing," Andrea said as she returned to the living room. She opened the front door for India and the rest of the kids to follow her outside.

Blue's grandmother returned to the living room. The frail, gray-haired woman in her late 70s asked if I wanted anything to drink. I said no thanks and sat down on her plastic covered burgundy couch.

Her small living room was cluttered with pictures and small religious statues of angels and the Virgin Mary. A 15-inch color TV sat on a wooden counter next to family photos and awards. I noticed the football and baseball trophies that Blue won while playing Little League sports in Dearborn as a young boy. There were also Army medals and a college diploma with the name Terrance Gray on it.

I'm sure Blue's grandmother rarely had company, so she took

the opportunity to talk about the awards and pictures of her family members that hung on the walls and sat on top of the wooden counter.

"You know, this is my youngest son," she said, holding a picture of a man in an Army uniform that looked as if it was taken in the early 1970s.

"He was a good boy. He never gave his mama any trouble. I thought he was gonna be the one child out of six that was really gonna do something special. He did do special things for a while. He went to the service. And then he went on to college and learned. He came out, got married and had my grandbabies, Terrence Jr. and India. He found himself a decent job. They were living good too. They had a nice house on the North Side. But the boy couldn't stay away from where he didn't need to be. He started hanging around old friends and got into those drugs. Then he got his wife on it and lord knows..."

She stopped talking, put the picture down and walked into the kitchen. Blue opened the bathroom door and I followed him into his room. As he brushed his fade, he looked at me and said, "It's about that time." I nodded in agreement and sat down in a chair as Blue left the room to get something from the kitchen. I laughed to myself as I saw Blue's 23s on the top of his dresser with a toothbrush next to them. Behind the shoes were car keys and a black notebook with a yellow No. 2 pencil in it. I opened the notebook to the page where the pencil was located and read.

The wound is closed but tha pain remains close/
Close enough to catch me when I'm runnin 2 slow/
Slowed by tha grief I can't release from below/
Below the devil's fire burning and won't let go/
My glow becomes ghost and gets darker wit each dose.

I turned to the next page and read more.

Itz all spread apart I'm tryin to piece together my reality/
My spirit tries to battle me and I'm losin all of my sanity/
I've seen bad scenes and it replayz drastikally/
My eyez can't hide I try 2 kill it until its half a dream....

"Hey, what's up man! What you doing Minus?" Blue said as he returned to his room and saw that his notebook was in my hand and open. I closed the notebook and placed it back on his dresser. Blue picked up the notebook, turned his head and gave me a look that I had never seen from him. It was a look of being exposed and vulnerable. Blue usually wore an unaffected and vicious look on his face. At that moment, I saw a vulnerable Blue. His shield was penetrated. His edge was gone. I no longer saw the boy people in the streets called Blue. For the first time since we met, I was staring at Terrance Gray Jr.

"How long have you been writing?" I asked.

"Not too long. I started after I visited my momma up in Lincoln a few months back," Blue said in a calm and straight forward voice as he thumbed through the notebook.

"Oh. I see."

"I mean, it was all hard for me when I was younger. Just wanting to come home from school and talk to my momma face to face. I use to hate going down to that jail and knowing that she couldn't come back home with me. So I stopped going to visit her for about four years. I finally went back to Lincoln with my grandma and India to see my momma on her birthday. India was a baby when my parents were arrested, so she really didn't understand what was happening. But the last time we went up there, she knew exactly what was going on. It tore me up to look in India's eyes when we had to leave that jail without my momma. That same day, I bought a notebook from the store and wrote my first poem when I got home. Before I knew it, I was writing something everyday. It's just how I get away for a minute. It's the only time I feel normal or relaxed. When I write, I'm under control. It moves a thousand miles per hour out there, and I have to move faster or I will get ran over."

"I hear you."

"You remember Nikki?" Blue leaned against the wall and looked out of his window at the Dearborn project's courtyard four stories below.

"Nakesa Hill from our seventh grade class, right?"

"Yeah. You know her momma is on that rock hard. She messed around and started buying right before the summer. She's like in her 40s or something. They say she got fired in June from her job for stealing. By the end of the summer, she started losing weight, lost her front teeth and started selling herself. Her lowest point was when she offered Nikki to a dealer named Duck to pay for some rock. She told Nikki that she would kick her out of their apartment if she didn't do what he wanted. I guess Nikki didn't have nowhere else to go. A few weeks back, Duck took her to a vacant apartment in the back of Dearborn. Wasn't no bed or nothing. Just a cold floor. Duck told Nikki to lay down. She laid down, closed her eyes and didn't say nothing. I usually don't let stuff like that get to me, but that just wasn't right.

I have to get India out of here. I can't have her around this mess as she gets older. It's two sides to this game and I can't control most of what's going on out there. But I can control what goes on in this notebook."

"Look, let's forget about Fat Na..."

"Man kill that. It's hard here. But while we here, we can't give them an excuse. Especially that dude Nate. You can give him one, but you better know that he's gonna try to get you again." Blue said as he threw his notebook on his bed and walked out of his room. He returned several minutes later with his edge intact. We both laid down a plan to get back at Fat Nate.

Through talks with people in the neighborhood, Blue found out that Fat Nate often hung out at Metcalfe Park. We decided to go there and get at him the best way we knew how.

Before leaving his room, Blue grabbed his leather jacket and reached under his bed. He pulled out an orange shoebox. Inside was a stack of money with a rubber band wound tightly around it, a dime bag and a black a weapon. Blue put the weapon in the small of his back and pulled his shirt down over it.

"You think we really need that?" I asked Blue as I pointed at his waist.

"Boy you must've forgot who Fat Nate is. Fat Nate don't care about nobody and he's known for holding heat. That big dude ain't going down without a fight," Blue said as he adjusted his belt buckle.

"My thing is to go down there, rough him up if I have to, and get my shoes back. I'm not trying to make this something that it's not."

"Joe, we going down into his territory where he lay his head. If we slip up, we won't make it out of there, I told you them Taylor boys don't play. I ain't going down there to use heat, but if Fat Nate and them other boys come wrong, we gotta be ready."

I knew that taking heat could bring heat, but protection was a must. Fat Nate and the rest of the boys from Robert Taylor needed to understand some things. They took an inch and I did not want them to think they would have a chance to take a mile.

Blue grabbed the car keys off his dresser and placed them in his pocket. We left his grandmother's apartment and headed to the parking lot where Blue walked to a brown 1980 Chevy Caprice and unlocked the doors. A hype who worked at the post office let him use the car in exchange for drugs. So instead of catching the public bus, Blue drove the Caprice to Metcalfe Park.

We arrived at the Park around 3 o'clock that afternoon. Fierce winds blew dust and loose trash across the park. The Robert Taylor Homes towered over the park that was covered by large patches of dirt and dead grass. Kids played in the scattered debris while a few teenagers worked to peddle drugs to a couple of hypes who trotted through the park. Blue and I took a moment to observe the movements of everyone in the park. It appeared to be an area used for low-end dealing. Once we figured out the setup, we began to search for Fat Nate. But after 20 minutes of searching, Fat Nate was nowhere in sight.

The neighborhood candy van pulled up as we stood near a bench. Several kids ran to the white van and pointed at the pictures of chips, candy and sodas. Blue noticed one boy who stood in front of the van and stared at the pictures while his friends bought potato chips and candy. Blue struck up a conversation with the boy who looked to be around 9 or 10-years-old.

"What's up little buddy? They make that stuff look good on them pictures don't they?" Blue asked the pudgy boy who wore a faded blue jacket and brown skull cap.

"Yeah," the boy responded as he wiped snot from his nose.

"What they call you out here?"

"Pee-Wee."

"Say Pee-Wee, do you know Fat Nate or Winky?"

"Yeah, they hanging with Rico and Lil Cory by the shed."

"Show me where the shed is."

The boy walked and we followed. He led us across a baseball field and pointed us in the direction of a wooden shed that was most likely used at one time for family barbeques. Now surrounded by trash and covered with graffiti, the shed was a hang out spot for the boys from the Robert Taylor Homes. Blue handed the boy a five dollar bill. The boy took the money, put it in his sock and ran towards the candy van.

Blue and I moved closer and noticed eight boys under the shed. We hid behind two trees as the boys under the shed talked and passed around a bottle that was concealed by a brown paper bag. It didn't take long for me to spot Fat Nate. He wore a red Chicago Bulls skull cap, a black bomber jacket and the 23s were untied on his feet. He sat on top of a table and chewed on a straw. A guy wearing a gray White Sox Starter jacket sat beside Fat Nate.

"Hey, Winky," another dude yelled to the guy wearing the White Sox jacket. "Pass that over here."

"Stop begging Rico. You the only hustler I know who begs like a bum. Makes me think that you smoking your own shit," the guy in the White Sox jacket yelled back as the other boys laughed.

"Don't make me get Ramon. You know you only got one more time to mess up with him Winky."

"Ramon be on some other stuff sometimes, Joe. He puts his hands in our pockets before we can put our own hands in 'em. That's why you gotta get those ends when you can catch it," Fat Nate said.

"Speaking of Ramon, I gotta go to the Hole and pick something up real quick. Come walk with me Fat Nate."

Although Blue had heat, we wanted to make sure that we didn't get too close to the shed. So we waited. Five minutes passed before Fat Nate and Winky left the shed and began walking towards the trees that Blue and I stood behind. We were completely out of their view as they approached.

Fat Nate and Winky carried on a loud conversation as they walked through the grass. I emerged from behind the tree and said, "What up, Nate?" Fat Nate's jaw dropped as he removed his hands from his pockets. Before he could react, I pounded my fist into his right eye. He swung back and punched me on my forehead as Winky made an attempt to grab me. Blue hit Winky in the nose and hit him again in the stomach.

I tripped Fat Nate, got on top of him, and punched him in his mouth and nose. I took the 23s off of his feet as Winky reached in his coat pocket and pulled out a switch blade. He attempted to stab Blue, but only nicked him with the blade. The other boys who were under the shed began running towards us. Blue pulled out his gun and began firing. Winky stumbled as he, Fat Nate and the other boys ran in the opposite direction. Blue shot twice more at Fat Nate and his boys. Those in the nearby area scattered as screams echoed throughout the park. Blue and I ran back to the Chevy Caprice. Blue tried to crank up the car and it stalled. He pumped the gas three times and turned the car's ignition. Nothing happened. I looked out of Blue's driver side window and saw Fat Nate and four other boys running in our direction.

"Hurry up!" I yelled to Blue as they got closer. One of the boys threw a brick at the car. Blue started the car and slammed his foot on the gas. As Blue drove away, the brick shattered the back window on the driver's side. The brick landed in the back seat and particles of glass hit my neck and shoulder. Blue sped away and five shots were fired in the direction of the car. We ducked our heads until we reached the Dan Ryan Expressway.

Sweat rolled down the side of my face as I gasped for air. I closed my eyes for a few seconds to calm down. I put my left hand over my face and rolled down the window. The 23s were in my lap. I wiped the sweat off of my forehead and took a look at the shoes. It was the first time I had laid eyes on them since I took them off of Fat Nate's feet. I peaked at the inside tongue. The tag read: US size 12.

CHAPTER 11

I think you've just crossed him. -Hassan Wright

Detectives are trying to find the person responsible for the shooting death of 12-year-old Sharonda Lanvale. Saturday around five o'clock p.m., Sharonda was shot once in the chest as she played with friends at Metcalfe Park. Witnesses say a group of young men began shooting after an altercation occurred. No suspects have been named.

"Honey, I tell you. These people out here are going crazy. They're out here killing little kids and doing all types of mess. They need to take these hoodlums off the streets and send them all to hell," my mom said in response to the Sunday afternoon news report at noon on Channel 5.

The egg sandwich that I ate 10 minutes prior to hearing the news was making its way to my throat. I stood up from the couch, ran into the bathroom and hurled inside of the toilet. After rinsing my mouth out, I filled my hands with warm water and splashed it on my face. I jumped in the shower and scrubbed with a towel until my skin was sore. Forty minutes of scrubbing in the shower did not cleanse me. Once I finished showering, I picked up the phone to call Blue.

"Hello," Andrea answered.

"Andrea, can you put Blue on the phone?"

"Child, I'm on the other line. You have to call him back later," Andrea said.

"Andrea! Before you hang up, my mom said they looking for new people at the hospital."

"Oh for real. You told her I was looking for work right?"

"Yeah, that's why I need to talk to Blue right now. She wants me to ask him a question about you."

"Hold on. 'Telephone Blue! Ms. Hall needs to ask you something about me. And you better put in a good word because you know I been looking for a job!'"

"Talk to me," Blue said after he grabbed the phone from Andrea.

"Did you watch the news today?" I asked.

"Naw, what happened?" he responded.

"Somebody got killed yesterday."

"That ain't nothing. That happens every day over here."

"No, at Metcalfe Park. A little girl."

"Damn! I have to get rid of it. I'm gonna hit you back later."

I waited by the phone while playing several games of Solitaire. After each game, I would stare at the receiver. I finished six games before the phone finally rung.

"Yo Blue, what you do with it?" I asked after picking up the receiver.

"This isn't Blue son, this is your grandmother."

"Oh, hey grandma."

"Listen son, you need to take a long look at yourself. Your mother told me how you've been getting in trouble at school. Your grandfather would not be proud of you right now."

"I know grandma, I'm going to get it together."

"You don't want to be like those fools out there on the corner wasting time drinking and smoking all day. I see little boys your age running around in the streets during school hours and I pray that I'll never see you out there with them."

"You won't grandma."

"I'm going to hold you to that son. Let me speak with your mother."

"Okay, hold on."

Once my mother and grandmother finished speaking, I sat on my bed with the phone beside me. I eventually closed my eyes while waiting for it to ring again. But Blue never called.

I woke up the following morning with the phone under my arm and playing cards stuck to my face. I removed the cards and called Blue to see if he had gotten rid of the weapon.

"Hello," Andrea answered the phone.

"Can I talk to Blue," I asked.

"Boy, why are calling here so much? We haven't seen Blue since he left the house yesterday. So I don't know where he is."

"Damn, alright."

"Minus, so what did your mother say about that job opening. Should I come down to the hospital?"

"Ahh, naw. She'll call you."

When I hung up the phone, I thought about going to Dearborn to find Blue. But with my past troubles at Dunbar, I could not afford to be late for school. I decided to take a shower and I walked to the bus stop while eating a Twinkie.

The school bus arrived at Dunbar High a half an hour before first period. While walking through the hallway, several students stared at me without speaking. But this time, their eyes were not on my shoes. Two upper classmen approached me before I entered my first period class. One of the boys bumped my right shoulder and my notebook fell to the floor. I reached down to pick up my notebook and the boy who bumped me said, "After school homeboy!"

I held my response after looking up and seeing my teacher standing near the classroom's entrance. I glanced back at the boys and figured they were down with Fat Nate and Winky.

Before going to second period, I went to my locker to grab my World History textbook. Once I opened my locker, I noticed a handwritten letter on top of my books.

"Yo Minus this Meathead. Come to the library right now bro. I got 2 tell u something. Serious bizness!"

I put the letter in my back pocket and closed my locker. I ran to the library so that I would have enough time to make it to second period without being late. When I opened the door to the library, I saw Meathead sitting in the corner with a newspaper in front of him as if he were reading.

"Man, are you looking at the pictures or something, because I never saw you touch a newspaper before," I said to Meathead in a loud whisper.

"Don't question my skills Minus, I know a lot."

"Whatever you say. Why did you bring me up here anyway? Do you need for me to teach you how to read?"

"Naw, I wanted you to come up here so that you could read between the lines."

"What lines?"

"All I know is that you are in some trouble bro. You kinda hot right now. Have you noticed that people have been looking at you funny lately?"

"Let them look. It's Fat Nate and his boys probably. But I can't worry about them."

"Only if it was just them."

"What do you mean?"

"I was walking with my cousin Derrick and his boys this morning before school. And your name popped up in the conversation. They were talking about how you and Blue went to Robert Taylor and shot the place..."

"Look, I didn't do anything!"

"I'm not the judge. I'm just telling you what I heard. Anyway, they are saying some big time boys from Robert Taylor is looking for you right now. I'm not just talking Fat Nate. They're saying some boys who really get after people. I told you to come in here because I can't be seen with you in the hallway. If I were you, I would go home now and hide under the bed. But you don't know me so I'm out, peace."

Meathead left the newspaper in his seat and walked to the door. Before leaving the library, he looked both ways to see if anyone was around. He then put his baseball cap on his head and walked into the hallway.

I removed the newspaper from the chair and sat down. Meathead would often exaggerate when he told stories. But this time, I had a feeling that he was not stretching the truth. There were people looking for me. And besides Fat Nate and Winky, I didn't have the slightest idea of who they were. The chances of me running into more trouble would increase the longer I remained at Dunbar. During second period class, I stood alone outside of the school and waited for the number 3 CTA bus to arrive.

While on the bus, I thought of speaking to someone who could bring some understanding to the situation. Discussing the problem with my mother would have caused her more stress. I considered talking to Larry, but his father was a detective and I was not sure if he would keep quiet. I needed advice from a person who could be trusted. I thought of Hassan.

I stepped off of the bus near Lil D's Barbershop. When I made it inside of the shop, most of the barbers were discussing the Chicago Bulls game from the night before. Hassan stopped cutting his client's hair, looked at me and said, "Minus, it's not even noon yet. Why aren't you in school?" I glanced around the shop and then asked Hassan if we could talk in private. He told me to hold tight until he finished working on his client.

Within 10 minutes, Hassan turned off his clippers, accepted his client's payment and we both walked to the meeting room that was located near the back of the barbershop.

"So what's going on young brother? Is there a problem?" Hassan asked as he brushed hair from his barber's apron.

"Problems can be solved, but I'm not sure if there is a way out of this," I confided after taking a seat at the table.

"How did you get there?"

"I bought some 23s a couple of weeks ago and I got caught in the wrong place with them. Saturday, I went after the boys who I thought took them. My homeboy and I went to Metcalfe Park to get back at the dudes. One thing led to another and shots were fired. A young girl ended up getting shot."

"Sharonda Lanvale?"

"Yeah, I think that's the name that was on the news."

"Did you shoot her?"

"I didn't have a gun, but my homeboy had one on him. But I don't have an idea where he is right now. And I just heard that some people from Robert Taylor are looking for me. That's why I had to leave school."

Hassan took off his apron and turned his back to me. He folded his arms and took a deep breath before speaking again.

"Have you ever heard of Ramon Lanvale?" Hassan asked.

"No, I don't think so," I replied.

"Well Ramon Lanvale is one of the biggest dealers in this city. He runs the Robert Taylor projects. Nothing comes in, or goes out without him knowing. I used to run with him when I stayed over there some years back. He can be dangerous if you cross him. And I think that you and your boy just crossed him because Sharonda Lanvale was his baby sister."

I folded my arms on the table and rested my forehead on my right wrist.

"Do you know if the police have been to your house yet?" Hassan asked.

"No. They haven't."

"That's a good and a bad thing. It's good that you're not caged up right now, but Ramon has this thing for putting the neighborhood on silence. He'll get the word out that he doesn't want any police involved. So no one will come forward and say anything about the shooting. But when there's a silence, he's going to go after you himself, before you have a chance to get arrested."

"Maybe I should just turn myself in, huh?"

"That could work, but chances are that it won't. Ramon has people on the inside that would be waiting for you to get there. At 15, they can try you as an adult and put you into the regular prison population. You are sure that you didn't have a gun, right?"

"One-hundred percent sure."

"I'll try to get in touch with Ramon to see if we can work something out. But I can't promise you anything. Ramon and I live in two different worlds now."

A mixture of sleet and snow began to fall as I left the barbershop and walked to the bus stop. With each second that passed, I attempted to take my thoughts off the issue. I rapped lyrics from Biz Markie and Kool G. Rap. I tried to think about Imani and the other fine girls at Dunbar in the shorts and skirts they wore when it was warm outside. And I recalled the last Bulls game when MJ dropped half a bill. Thinking of other things provided brief relief, but my mind was back on the problem as I stepped on the CTA bus.

I sat alone in the back of the bus and tried to figure how my reality had changed in a matter of hours. In two days, I went from being a freshman at Dunbar High to being involved in the murder of a young girl. I could have let the whole thing go from the start. The day that I lost those shoes should have been the day that I forgot about them. I will always regret the fact that I did so little to stop Blue from taking that gun from his shoe box. But what I regret more was that I didn't stop myself from going after Fat Nate.

I slept for over three hours once I returned home. Shortly after five o'clock in the afternoon, my mom charged into my room with her coat on her back and a black purse under her left arm.

"What's wrong Minus, are you sick or something? You've been sleep since I came home from work," my mom asked.

"Naw, I'm just tired today. I got a lot of stuff on my mind."

"Well, if you're just tired, you need to go to sleep when it gets dark outside. I let you get away with it yesterday, but you know there's no sleeping under my roof during the daytime. It's not snowing anymore, so I'm on my way to the store to get groceries because I have to work a double tomorrow. There are two bags of garbage in the kitchen that need to be taken out now. So get up and do some homework when you get back in!"

After rolling out of the bed, I placed a black White Sox hat on my head and pulled the brim low so that my eyes were barely visible. With two bags of trash in my hand, I unlocked the front door and walked to the dumpster. I swung the bags into the dumpster and jogged back to my apartment. As I approached the red steps, someone with a soft voice called my name. I turned to my left and saw Meta walking with a younger boy in my direction. She said that she was on her way to visit her aunt who stayed down the street from me. We began to talk and a black Chevy Monte Carlo with tinted windows pulled up in front of my apartment. Someone rolled down the passenger side window and hollered, "THAT'S HIM RIGHT THERE!" The car sped off leaving tire marks on the pavement. Meta told the boy, who I later found out was her brother, to walk to her aunt's place without her. Meta waited until she saw that her brother had made it to the steps of her aunt's apartment. I invited Meta inside so that no one else would recognize me on those steps.

Meta sat on the couch and examined our apartment. She then unzipped her purse and fiddled inside as if something of importance was buried at the bottom of it. I leaned against the wall and chewed on my nails before retying my shoe. Nearly five minutes passed and no words were exchanged. Meta broke the silence by pointing at a picture on the wooden coffee table and asking, "Is that your father?" It was a black-and-white photo of my grandfather holding his trumpet in a three-piece suit.

"Naw, I don't know my real dad. That's my grandfather. Probably the greatest man I've ever met."

"Um, he's cute for an older man. You two have the same smile, except you don't smile as much anymore."

"I guess nothing is really funny. I wish I could talk to my grandfather now though. He had the answers to everything." I said as I turned towards the wall and began staring at a picture of my grandfather and me at the lake.

"Where is he?"

"He passed five years ago."

"Oh, I'm sorry."

"No need to apologize."

"You know, you can still talk to him. I mean, I know he's no longer here with you, but he will always be a part of you. Just like my older cousin, Teresa will always be a part of me. She died a few years back. It had something to do with a jealous boyfriend. She was a cheerleader. That's why I decided to be a cheerleader. She sung in a singing group, so I wanted to sing in a group. But my vocal cords weren't really made for singing and that didn't last too long. And she went to Hampton University, so I'm going to Hampton once I graduate. Whenever there's something on my mind and no one is around for me to talk to, I talk to her. I think about what she would say to me. I'm not saying that all of my problems are solved, but talking to her helps me to feel better."

Meta stood up from the couch and placed her hand on my shoulder and said, "I'm sorry about what happened between us.

I wished things didn't go the way they did."

"There's a reason why things go the way they go. Sometimes it takes a while to see it. But there's a reason," I said as I continued to stare at the picture.

"So what do we do now? Do we start over?"

"Naw, we can't start over. The only thing that we can do is try to get through now and hope to make it to whatever is next."

Meta grabbed my hand and pulled me in closer for a hug. I told her that I needed time to think about some things and walked her to the door. After I opened the door, she gave me a peck on the cheek and then kissed my lips. As she moved away, she looked me in the eyes and said, "I believe in you Minus. I hope you believe in me."

Chapter 12

If you play in the devil's playground, you have to pay for the priviledge. -Ramon Lanvale

The ring of the telephone woke me from my slumber a few minutes after 10 p.m. I grabbed the beige push-button phone on my nightstand and answered the call. A muffled voice and static made it hard to figure out who was on the other end of the line. But I soon figured that it was Hassan when he mentioned the discussion that we had earlier in the barbershop.

"He said that he'll meet with you," Hassan uttered matter-of-factly.

"Who is 'He?'"

"He is the guy you need to see. And right now, there's no way around this."

"So what day?"

"It's more like what time. He wants to meet with you right now."

"Now? It's almost 11 o'clock on a school night. My mom

is already buggin' about me coming home late and getting in trouble at Dunbar. And I left school early today so Mr. Franks is probably going to call her tomorrow. I'm not trying to get in deeper trouble."

"Brother, I'm all about the rules and I commend you on your desire to follow them. But if ever there was a time to not be the good son, this is it. It won't be a great ending if he has to look for you. I'll be there in 20 minutes."

I hung up the phone and walked to my mother's room. The TV was on, but she was fast asleep under the covers. I walked back to my closet and grabbed a brown coat and black skull cap. Without turning on the lights, I tiptoed into the living room with my sneakers in my right hand and looked out of the window onto the street. Eight minutes before 11, Hassan arrived and parked in front of my apartment. I twisted the front door knob and shut it slowly behind me. Once I reached the entrance door to my apartment building, I put on my sneakers. I walked down the red steps and turned to see if all of the lights were still off in my apartment. The only light came from the television in my mother's room. I opened the passenger door of Hassan's Volvo station wagon and looked back at my apartment as he put his car in gear.

"Peace be unto you. How do you feel about this?" Hassan asked as he drove off.

"I don't know what to feel," I replied.

"Hopefully, it will be better tomorrow."

"Yeah, tomorrow."

Hassan stopped at a red light two blocks from my apartment. We were approached by a man who wore a partially torn Chicago Bears sweatshirt, dirty jeans and held a spray bottle and rag in his right hand. The man began to spray Hassan's front windshield and wiped the spray off with his rag.

"Fellas, I got a good deal going tonight. I'll clean this for only 10 dollars," the man said as he sprayed more water on the windshield and wiped.

"I'm OK brother. I don't need my windows cleaned tonight," Hassan said.

"Alright, I'll take five dollars. This won't take no time at all. How about two dollars? Come on man, throw me some-thing!"

Hassan reached behind himself and grabbed a V8 juice and banana from the back seat. He handed it to the man and the guy opened the container and took a swig from the bottle. The man cringed at the taste and slammed the bottle to the ground. He then threw the banana into Hassan's car and walked back to the sidewalk. Hassan shook his head and continued driving after the light turned green.

"This is what has happened." Hassan said as he got on the Dan Ryan Expressway.

"What you mean?"

"All of what is around us is much bigger than what we are seeing. Put a bunch of people in a small area that has more liquor stores than health centers, more dealers than fathers, and hardly any jobs or legit ways to make decent money. Nobody likes where they are, so deep down, we began to hate everything and everybody that's around us. And this self-hate has somehow become a part of how we think and what we have become."

Hassan was speaking the truth, but the truth did little to al-leviate my fear of not knowing what was ahead. He could sense that it was getting the best of me. So he stopped talking, reached into the side pocket of his door, grabbed a tape cassette and inserted it in the stereo.

The sounds of Eric B. and Rakim allowed me to escape for a few minutes. Rakim's vivid wordplay was always worthy of the rewind button. The way he flowed over break beats with rhyme schemes that painted pictures of his block took me to the big NY without leaving the Chi. I could imagine the streets of New York when he spit. And in a weird way, I also saw the South Side. His lyrics showed a struggle that was happening in every hood in America. He let it be known that no matter where you were from, the politics of the streets were basically the same.

Three songs played before Hassan ejected the tape. I reverted back to that same uneasy feeling as he turned into the Robert Taylor Homes. The Robert Taylor Homes looked like a miniature city with more than two dozen 16-story buildings spanning for as many blocks and towering over us as we drove in semi-darkness. It took Hassan nearly 10 minutes to drive from the entrance of the projects to the south end. He turned off his headlights and parked his car in what was known as The Hole.

The Robert Taylor Homes were notorious, but the Hole was probably the closest that a human could get to hell without dying. I recalled overhearing stories of the Hole from thugs who stayed in Dearborn. Criminals with long rap sheets talked about it as a place where they would not walk alone. For a while, the postal service did not allow its workers to deliver mail there. The ambulances and even the police stayed away unless there was a catastrophe.

It was almost midnight with nearly two inches of snow on the ground, and the Hole was as busy as a normal business day on Division Street. Hassan and I stepped out of the car and watched as crackheads and heroin fiends moved about clutching money in their hands. The hypes resembled characters from the *Night of the Living Dead* as they whizzed by us to reach the dealers. Dope dealers that wore 23s and starter coats hustled to provide for the hypes.

But it wasn't the simple hand-to-hand deals that I was used to seeing in Dearborn. The boys in the Hole had it set up like an advanced operation. There were several pitchmen who would try to persuade the hypes by yelling, "I got that Glow. I got that Bruce Leroy for ya!" "We got that Michael Jackson. That real *Thriller* over here!" Once they got the hype's attention, the pitchman would point the hype in the direction of another dealer. That dealer would take the hype's money and give it to a runner who took the money into one of the apartments in the high-rise. The hype would then walk behind one of the high-rise buildings where he could collect his dope in secret.

Hassan and I entered one of the high-rise buildings where nine dudes were gathered in the small lobby. Four boys stood together at the entrance and talked as five others leaned calmly against a wall near the elevator shaft. They all fell silent and stared at us as we approached. One of the dudes removed his hands from his pockets and began to rub his fist and pop his knuckles. Another reached inside his mouth and pulled out a small razor blade and held it tightly in his right hand. I kept my hands to my side and stared at the ground. Hassan broke the silence and said, "You brothers be safe." We made our way to the stairs and began to walk up 10 flights.

The staircase was polluted with empty beer cans, brown paper bags, broken bottles, plastic cups, used condoms, empty weed and crack sacks, and vials. Water that leaked from a busted pipe filled the stairway causing our shoes to get wet. The smell of urine stung my noise as I tried hard not to inhale. The walls were spray-painted with graffiti and the old chipped paint held on to the mildew and rust. We were greeted on the 10th floor by the sounds of babies crying, loud arguments and echoes from the closed-door apartments. A man who looked to be in his late 40s was asleep in the hallway with a bottle of liquor under his right arm.

Hassan stopped at an apartment where a tall hefty guy stood in front of the door with his arms folded. He looked at us but did not say a word. He unfolded his arms and put his right hand near his waist. Before the guy reached further, Hassan said, "Hey, brother, could you tell Ramon that Nardo is out here? The big guy walked into the apartment and shut the door. Seconds later, he reopened the door and allowed us to go inside.

The apartment was almost bare. No pictures or posters were on the walls. No paintings, statues or awards from past achievements. There was no couch. Four metal chairs were in front of a large floor model TV that had a Nintendo and VCR hooked up to it. There was one table in the kitchen with two large black plastic garbage bags on top of it. As we were waiting for Ramon, one of the runners came in and placed another full garbage bag on the table and ran back out of the apartment. Another guy grabbed all three of the plastic bags and put them into one of the rooms in the back. It was obvious that there was no trash in those bags, and no one really called that place home.

A tall, slender man wearing a white buttoned-up shirt with black slacks and shinny black hard-bottomed shoes emerged from one of the bedrooms. If he was in another area of the city, he could have probably passed for a college student or one of those downtown execs. He walked closer and I noticed that he looked familiar. I thought back and recognized him as the man who stepped out of the BMW and entered Mitchell's the first day that I visited Lil D's Barbershop. He was the guy with the power. He was the guy who literally owned the Robert Taylor Homes. He was Ramon Lanvale.

Ramon looked at Hassan and said, "Long time no see Nardo. Or should I say Brother Hassan, the self-righteous one?" They shook hands and hugged.

"Hassan will do. I see you have a new staff up here." Hassan said, slightly tilting his head towards the front door.

"You know how this business goes Hassan. The Five-O is gonna take a few of them, half might snitch, some get caught in the wrong place and the others are just not built for this. So every six months or so, we bring in a few new faces. Some of the new ones get what we're doing, most of them don't. It's not like when I had you out here to keep those middle managers and rookies in line. It took us some time. But boy, we made something out of nothing didn't we?"

"Yeah. We did Ramon. But ah, this is Minus. He is the young brother who was at the park the other day."

Ramon stepped away from Hassan and turned his back. He turned back around and said, "Thanks, Brother Hassan. I'd like for you to wait outside." Hassan looked at me and said, "Everything is cool Minus. I'll be right outside this door." Hassan opened the front door of the apartment and shut it behind him. I stared at the white front door hoping that Hassan would return. But the door remained closed and for the second time in my life, I actually felt the possibility of death.

Ramon stood in front of me with his hands in his pockets and looked at me with a scowl that shredded any ounce of confidence that remained. The harshness in his eyes caused my hands to shake. I fixed my head towards the floor and looked up only when his feet moved.

Ramon remained silent. He reached inside of his right pants pocket. I took one step backwards. On the inside of his right hand was a stick of gum. He opened the wrapper and placed the gum in his mouth before pointing to one of the metal chairs. I sat down in the chair and he began to pace slowly back and forth while looking at the ceiling. He exhaled and then began to speak.

"You know, today I had to go to the funeral home and make plans for Sharonda." A runner who barged into the room with another large plastic bag interrupted Ramon. Ramon became furious, "Shut that door Rico and tell Dre don't let nobody else in!" The runner put the bag on the floor and exited as quickly as he entered. Ramon put his hand over his face, gathered himself and began talking again.

"See I don't think you know anything about making it cause you probably a regular knucklehead who don't have anything to look forward to. But Sharonda was my family's pride. She was going to be the one who went to college to become a doctor, or the CEO of her own business. She was the only child my mother had who could've played a different game with different rules. She wasn't gonna be like me, or my other brothers and sisters. She had hope. But she can't do nothing now because she's dead. See drugs are not messing up these streets. True, it's messing up individuals. See what's messing up the streets is cats who are going around shooting just because they can pull a trigger. Y'all not doing this for territory or to gain something big. Y'all shooting just to get a name or so people will know you got some nuts. That makes you worse than a hype or crooked cop because you serve no purpose out here. We don't need you.

"But Hassan tells me that you didn't shoot Sharonda. I have to believe what Hassan says because he's always been a straightforward man. He took a bullet that was meant for me, so I will always owe him. He wants me to spare your life. I probably could do that, but there's something that has to be done. Although you did not shoot Sharonda, your homeboy did. And in my eyes, you are as guilty as your homeboy because you were there with him. So somebody has to go. It's either him or both of y'all. I suggest you make it him. I want you to be responsible for doing it. I want you to understand what this brings. I want you to have to live with it. If you play in the devil's playground, you have to pay for the priviledge. And this is one of the priviledges"

Ramon called Dre into the room. Dre pulled his shirt up, reached into his waistband and handed me a weapon. I grabbed it and moved towards the front door. As I opened the door, Ramon said, "I'm giving you one day." I put the weapon in my pants and did not look back. I made it out of that apartment alive, but I walked away without a conscience.

CHAPTER 13

You don't get that hour back. - Calvin Royals

It was four o'clock in the morning and my eyes were fixed on the ceiling in my room. With my hands clutched firmly behind my head, I laid on top of my twin-sized bed and searched for the answers to fragmented questions. The words of Ramon Lanvale dominated my thinking and stuck in my mind like a bad jingle. There had to be consequences to what took place, but the ultimatum Ramon gave me seemed worse than death.

Exits did not exist on the road that I was traveling on. I considered turning myself in to the police with the hopes of dodging the assignment I had been given. But I thought better of hiding inside the long arms of the law. The Chicago Police Department could not protect me from what I was up against. I had to follow Ramon's law or write a death sentence to be signed by the man himself.

The other problem was Fat Nate and Winky. Once Blue fired bullets, the game became a different sport. We could no longer battle with fists and be satisfied with the outcome. Guns were now involved. Fat Nate and Winky had reason to retaliate. Ramon was looking, but they were probably watching closer.

The puzzle was undone and it seemed as if a thousand small pieces were scattered. I had few options and very little time to make a decision. I weighed the potential danger. Fat Nate and Winky could do harm, but Ramon had the power to bring Hell to my front door. My mother was not going to pay for a mistake that my friend made. I was down to only one option. Blue had to go and I was going to be the one to send him.

"Talk to me," Blue answered the phone at 8 a.m. with a deep gruff voice.

"What's up Blue?" I asked.

"Ain't nothing. About to get up and out in a minute. The Five haven't stopped by your house have they?"

"Naw, have you seen them?"

"Not my way. But I gotta feeling they might be looking. So I'm not going to the hustle, I'll probably lay low at the spot."

"You get rid of it?"

"Pretty much."

"So, what's happening on your end?"

"Same mess, just a different can."

"Oh, I forgot to tell you. Before I made it to Dearborn the other day, I went to get some chips from the store and I saw Tanisha Smith."

"Tanisha from our 6th grade class?"

"Yeah man."

"Aw man. Is she still fine?"

"You know it. She looks even better now that she has a

shape on her."

"I remember when I used to dare you to kiss her cheek during P.E."

"I did it though. And you still owe me one dollar for doing it."

"It took your scary self about two months to do it. And when you finally did it, she gave you a good beat down," Blue reminded me as both of us laughed.

"Man, those were some of the best days of my life. I thought those times would never end."

"Everything gotta end, Minus," Blue said in a serious tone.

"I guess you're right. What's up for later on?"

"No telling. Why you ask? I thought your momma was putting the clamps on you during school nights."

"Oh, yeah. You know she's working kind of late so it's whatever until she gets home. But um, you think we can meet up?"

"I guess. What time?"

"Probably a little late. Is six o'clock cool?"

"Yeah, just come to the spot."

I hung the phone up and exhaled. I looked toward the floor and stared at the 23s that were against my wall in the corner. I thought about all that I went through to get them. There was an addiction to the chase of 23s and everything that came with owning a pair of the greatest shoes ever made. For one day, I was above every person who was around me. No one was better than me at that moment. I was ahead of my time and the 23s were the reason. It all produced an emotional high that became the center of my life. That high was taken away and I made myself believe that my life would be nothing without it. I yearned to get them back without knowing what it would bring back. I paid $110 for a pair of sneakers, but they were costing me my soul.

I got dressed as if I was going to school shortly after I got off of the phone with Blue. My mother was preparing to work a 12-hour shift and didn't leave the apartment until 8:30 a.m. To make her think that I was on my way to school, I walked outside with a folder and an Algebra book under my right arm. I stood on the corner of my block until I figured that she caught the bus to work. After 9:30, I returned to my apartment and waited until it was time for Blue and I to meet.

I poured a glass of orange juice, walked into my room and hung my coat on a hanger in the closet. In the corner of my closet was the old basketball I played with when I was younger. The ball was flat and the black lines and rubber grip was completely worn. Dirt had given the once orange ball a brownish hue. It caused me to recall my first encounter with Blue, Fat Nate and the world outside my front door. I often wondered what my life would be like if I had remained inside when that ball rolled down those steps.

The hours passed like seconds. For the remainder of the day, I stared out my bedroom window and watched as snow flurries fell on the sidewalk and street. Around five o'clock, two young boys ran through the snow with chips and sodas in their hands. They were eager to get to wherever they needed to be. In a way, I saw myself and Blue in those two youngsters. Blue was always down to do what it took to handle what needed to be done. When I gave him the call, he came to my defense. Somehow, that was not enough to steer me away from satisfying the revenge of Ramon Lanvale.

I took hold of my grandfather's horn and cupped my right

hand in the three o' clock position. I placed my lips on the mouthpiece and my fingers on the valves of the horn. From the bottom of my lungs, I blew air into the instrument. I pressed each valve as if I was squeezing life from the trumpet. High notes screamed from the instrument the faster I blew. My palms became greasy. Sweat trickled down my cheeks. The tension that was released through my lips had no boundaries or control. My jaws filled with pain as each vivid note escaped into the air. The music was a cry for help, but no one could hear. So I allowed myself to drown in the trumpet's moan of desperation.

I exhaled deeply after removing the trumpet from my lips. I tossed the trumpet on the bed, put on my coat, skull cap and black hooded sweatshirt. Ramon's gun was in a book bag directly under my bed. I grabbed the gun, took out the clip and counted the bullets. Halfway filled, I reinserted the clip and placed the gun in the waistband of my jeans. I locked the front door to my apartment and walked out of my building. As I stood at the top of the red steps, I pulled the hood over my head and walked with a slow stride in the direction of Dearborn Homes.

Gray clouds gave way to the darkness of night. Snow was no longer falling and the evening winds were smothering all who roamed Dearborn Street. But the coldness of the night could not match the freeze that developed in my heart. The mission outweighed the consequences. There was no room for concern. With a weapon in my waist, I was prepared to use of it on a person who I once considered my closest friend.

The residents fussed and yelled, cars sped by bumping music, and the dealers called out the products that they had to offer the hypes. The common sounds in Dearborn were as loud as ever, but the noise did not exist to me. My senses were numb.

I moved at a steady pace through the projects. I only stopped when I reached the apartment building that Blue called the spot. I kept my hands in my pockets and looked up to the third floor window which shown throughout the dimly lit apartment. I clutched the handle of the gun and took one step forward before my focus was lost.

Out of the corner of my left eye, I saw C-Roy emerge from behind the apartment building with another hype. He wore a dingy DePaul University jacket, black jeans and half of a cigarette hung from the side of his mouth. I tilted my head towards the right, coughed up phlegm and spit it on the sidewalk and continued to walk.

"Hey, uh Minus!" C-Roy called out my name and began jogging towards me as the other hype headed in another direction. I turned my back to him, but he continued to follow me in an effort to get my attention. As he got closer, he grabbed his chest and sucked in air. He stood up straight and recognized the anger in my eyes. He was the last person I wanted to see. He was the last person who needed to be in front of me at that moment.

"If you're mad, you have every right to be. Our first meeting should've been better than what it was. It just caught me offguard."

"Look man, I don't have anything to say to you right now. I really suggest that you keep walking to wherever you have to be." I told C-Roy as I moved away from him. He followed me and reached out to grab my right shoulder. I jerked away and he noticed the bulge under my sweatshirt. He took two steps backwards and looked at me with a still face as we stood directly in front of each other. With both of his hands in the air he said, "I just wanna rap for a minute. That's all."

I covered the bulge of the gun with my jacket as he began to speak.

"I'm not gonna stand here and tell you how I should've been there all those years cause that really don't matter right now. But you at least need to know who I am so you can know who you are."

"Man, I'm nothing like you!"

"Yeah you right. You ain't nothing like me. See I was the man when I was your age. I owned my first car at 15. All types of broads was on my shoulder. And I ran the West Side like I was President Carter. But things changed before I could get ready. A little bit after your momma had you, I got locked up for seven years on a drug charge. When I got out, the whole game was different. It wasn't just powder and smack no more. Crack came in hard. The players were new and all the people who I came up with were locked up or strung out. Times got rough and I tried it. It's been bad ever since. But when I was locked up, I learned something worth keeping. The prison has this thing that they do called 23-and-1. They lock you down for 23 hours in confinement. They leave you alone in your cell until the 23rd hour. When that finally comes, you have one hour to do what you gotta do. You have one hour to make sense out of that day. After that hour is gone, your day is over. You don't get that hour back. You don't get that day back. You have time Minus. Don't wait until the 23rd hour. You have to make your life mean something now."

C-Roy glanced at my waist and shook his head. He zipped up his jacket and walked away. A dealer approached C-Roy and said, "C-Roy, I got them meds for ya." C-Roy removed the cigarette from his mouth and continued without acknowledging the dealer. I watched him as he passed three hypes who stood together and laughed while drinking from liquor bottles that were again concealed in brown paper bags. They all spoke to C-Roy with the hopes that he would join them. C-Roy nodded and said, "What's up," but continued to walk as if he were no longer interested in being a part of their world.

I stood alone in front of the high-rise where Blue's vacant apartment was located. I took the hood off my head and walked to a sewage drain. I reached into the waistband of my jeans and grabbed the gun. The street lights reflected off the black .380 like newly shined dress shoes. I released the clip and threw the bullets and the gun into the sewage drain. With Ramon's gun no longer on me, I turned around and began to walk home.

"Where you going? I thought we were supposed to meet," Blue shouted as he walked from the entrance of the high-rise wearing a Bears Starter coat and a white sweatshirt.

"Oh, um yeah. I thought I forgot something but it ain't nothing." Blue hurried towards me. He was focused and looking through my eyes to see the truth. Our phone conversation must have given him a clue of why I was there. He picked up on my vibe and knew that I was there to kill him. I had forgiven myself for even considering the thought, but things had gone too far for him to do the same.

I balled my fists as he approached. He put his right hand behind his back as if he was reaching for something in his pants. I saw a brick on the ground and lunged towards it. Blue stopped and looked up. The sounds of police sirens were blaring through the projects. The dealers scattered and the hypes stood still. Three squad cars pulled directly in front of the high-rises and surrounded Blue and I. The police headlights beamed in our direction as the cops stepped out of their patrol cars.

"Stop whatever you're doing and put your hands on top of your heads!" One cop yelled as four other police officers jumped out of their cars with guns drawn. I put my hands on top of my head and kneeled down. They ordered us to lay face down on the pavement with our hands spread apart. I glanced over to Blue and saw that he was still standing.

"Put your hands on top of your head!" The police yelled at Blue as a small crowd began to gather behind the squad cars. Blue stood in the same position and looked directly at the police as they continued to shout orders. I turned in Blue's direction and told him to get down. Blue glanced at me and then looked back at the officers who stood in front of him.

"Get down? Get down? I ain't getting down for these bastards! See they'll come over here when it's time to cuff us up. But where the hell they at when all this other stuff is going on? Huh? Tell me that. Where the hell y'all at when these bullets be flying out here every night? Where the hell was y'all when they stole from my grandma and I was too young to help? I ain't getting down. Forget that!"

Blue held his position as the police continued to yell at him to get down. Moments later, Larry's father arrived in a grey unmarked car. Detective Murray wore a long beige trench coat over a black business suit. He took off his brim hat and walked closer to get a better view. He realized that it was Blue and I who were the suspects.

"Put down your guns! Put down your guns! I know these young men," he told the other officers as they all withdrew their weapons. Detective Murray walked slowly toward Blue and stood halfway between him and the other police. He turned towards the police and looked at them with assurance as he began to talk to Blue.

"You know we can do this the right way Terrance."

"Ain't no right way."

"I've been knowing you since you were a little boy. I know it feels like the world is against you, but you have to think right now. Those officers over there won't hesitate to kill you. So I suggest you follow me and it'll all be over."

"It ain't gonna ever be over Mr. Murray. None of this mess. Can't you see? They don't care about us. They don't care about anybody over here. So why should I care? They don't know anything about me. I don't have nothing. This is all I got!"

Blue reached in the small of his back and began to pull something out. Detective Murray screamed, "Hold your fire!" The officers ignored his command and began to fire bullets at Blue. I placed my forehead on the ground and covered the back of my head with both arms. I could hear the whistle of the bullets as they passed me. The bullet shells hit the icy pavement and sounded like quarters dropping on concrete. The police stopped firing.

Detective Murray grabbed me and rushed me into the direction of where the squad cars were. I looked back and saw Blue lying motionless in a pool of blood. The composition notebook where he wrote his poetry was a few inches away from his right index finger.

CHAPTER 14

I think I'm ready to say goodbye. —Minus Hall

I was arrested on suspicion of the murder of Sharonda Lanvale. The correctional officers at the Cook County Jail took my fingerprints, photo and issued me an 11-digit DOC ID number. I was given an orange uniform and escorted by two male officers to the Division 5 section of the jail. They walked me down a long dim hallway with white metal doors on each side. The officers stopped in the middle of the hallway and unlocked the holding cell. One officer took off the handcuffs and placed me in a cell with 10 other inmates. Most of the inmates appeared older than me and some were twice my size. The cramming of so many bodies in such a small space caused the cell to appear to be a bit smaller than a restroom at a fast-food restaurant. The stench was a mixture of underarm musk and urine. I breathed through my mouth in order to avoid inhaling the odor through my nostrils. The walls were cemented and covered by white paint that was beginning to peel. There was a small silver-plated sink that stood next to a white toilet that had smeared feces around the edges. There was a bench and bed made of metal that was cushioned with a thin cotton mattress.

Several conversations stopped as I entered the cell. Each inmate looked in my direction and sized me up. I made direct eye contact, but I kept my mouth closed as I found a place to stand in the crowded cell. After a few minutes passed, all eyes were off of me and the loud conversations continued. I stood up against the wall and was approached by a stocky dude who looked to be in his early 20s. Tattoos covered both of his arms like sleeves. His hair was partially twisted and he had a gold cap on his upper front tooth.

"What they call you home boy?"

"Minus."

"Oh yeah? I'm B-Cap. I'm from the Wild Hunneds. Where you from?"

"I'm from off of West 26th near Dearborn."

"Aww man, I got some people over there in Dearborn. What you claimin'?"

"I don't claim brah. I'm just trying to get through it."

"You gonna have to claim something. They ain't gonna let you do it in here by yourself. I'm down with this here for life," B-Cap said as he twisted his fingers to represent his set.

"What you in here for Minus?"

"A whole bunch of ongoing mess. You know how it be."

"You can talk homeboy, I ain't the Fedz."

"Yeah, I know. Why they got you down here?"

"This Lil sucker tried to play me. Kept dodging me and stuff because he owed me money. He was trying to get over so I had to pop him twice."

"How much he get you for?"

"He owed me a dub. It wasn't about the money though. It was the principle of it."

Moving around in the cell was barely an option. There were no books or newspapers to occupy our minds, so the conversations were the only form of diversion. Some inmates argued about who came from the roughest neighborhood while others talked about how they were facing bogus charges. A few sat quietly and thought of ways to get released and some joined fellow gang members to form a coalition. My hunger increased and I figured that I would be able to eat anything that was placed in front of me. But they served us rotten bologna sandwiches with old meat, stale cheese and molded bread. The only item that was worth consuming was the carton of lukewarm apple juice.

I fought hard against sleep. With so many inmates in one cell, I felt that falling asleep without one eye open could be disastrous or even fatal. Most of the inmates slept on the floor while others slept standing up against the walls. I stood up and closed my eyes, but never went to sleep. I would take five to 10 minute catnaps and made sure that I didn't drift into a deep sleep by doing 15 push-ups after each nap.

At seven o'clock the next morning, a pair of correctional officers grabbed me and two other inmates, and handcuffed us to each other. I figured I was going to see the judge, but the officers only placed us in another holding cell. This cell was set up just like the other one. Ten inmates jockeyed to claim a few inches for themselves in the cell. One person who was able to reserve a space on the bench was Tony. I recognized Tony from selling with Blue in Dearborn. After the officer unlocked the handcuffs, I walked over to Tony.

"Minus, they knocked down on you too huh?" Tony

asked as he stood up and gave me dap.

"Man, a lot went down in Dearborn the other night."

"Yeah, I know how it be. I just heard about what happened to Blue from my cousin Tay. It's messed up, Joe. That's my boy too. See the police is keeping the streets hot. They got a white boy taking Sawyer's spot so they laying everybody on the concrete right now. Trying to send a message and shit. But give it a couple of months. Daley talking all high and mighty, but soon as he gets comfortable, we right back where we started. Making money while they pretend to act like they care to stop it."

"I guess when they want you, they get you. I've been in here for a day and I thought they were taking me to see a judge. They took me out of the cell at seven o'clock this morning just to take me to another cell."

"Oh, they just trying to break you. They sending you through Bullpen Therapy. What they do is move you around to different cells to mess with your head. By the time you see the judge, you're so tired of being in the holding cells they figure that you'll give in."

If it was a game, they were playing the hell out of it and winning. I could barely stand as my eyes weakened. It was hard for me to comprehend what was going on around me. The cell walls moved and the inmates looked as if they grew two heads and three arms. The hours of standing without sleep had caught up with me. I managed to close my eyes for 20 minutes until I was, again, pulled out of the cell.

I was placed in handcuffs and escorted into an interrogation room. The room was dim and uncomfortable. We were deep into February, but the air conditioning was blasting as if it were the hottest day of the summer. I sat alone in the room for nearly 30 minutes. Finally, the door opened. and two detectives walked in.

A black detective, who looked to be in his late 40s, walked into the room first followed by a white detective who appeared to be a few years younger. The black detective was a heavy-set guy with a thick beard and bald head. The white detective was slim with hair slicked back like the Fonz from "Happy Days." While the black detective opened a folder and reviewed a police report, the white detective offered me a Sprite. I took the soda and began to drink. "Taste good don't it?" The black detective asked.

"I guess. I mean it's just Sprite. Nothing special."

"Well, remember that taste. Soon you gonna be drinking toilet water and living with some big dude named Bubba. You know we have witnesses who say you killed Sharonda Lanvale."

"I never killed anyone."

"Where do you stay?"

"You know everything, you tell me."

"Everybody needs an ass, but this place right here don't have room for smart ones. So answer the damn question before this foot here starts searching for a butt to kick."

"West 26th."

"You were at Taylor Park on the day that Sharonda was killed. Am I correct?"

"I'm not sure."

"I think you are sure. You stay off West 26th. What were you doing all the way over there at Taylor Park?"

"I don't hang out over there. That's not my hood."

"The word is that you went over there to get some shoes. And it's all beginning to make sense now. Some of the boys from Taylor Park took your shoes and you wanted revenge. You went back and shot up the place cause you gotta let them know you ain't a punk right? But while you were shooting at them, you ended up killing a little girl. Now explain to me everything that happened in a way that a three year-old could understand."

"I told you, I've never killed anybody."

"You know what. Your kind makes me sick. See I go to neighborhoods like yours, and the brothers — no I can't call them that because they're not related to me. I mean those ignorant assholes will look at me and call me an Uncle Tom because I wear my pants above my waist and speak correct English. But I'm not the Uncle Tom. It's Negroes like you who are the real Toms. You're the ones who give hard working black people like me a bad name."

"You don't know anything about me."

The black detective threw his folder down and slapped the soda can out of my hand. He charged at me with his right fist balled. The white detective grabbed his arm and pulled him back.

"You're gonna pay for that murder you little bastard. You're gonna pay!" The black detective yelled as the white detective took him out of the room in an attempt to calm him down. They both returned seconds later. The white detective pulled up a chair next to me and started to talk.

"I'm not concerned with all this black and white talk, because the way I see it is that people are people and they're bound to make mistakes. I remember when I was a young boy and my mom bought this vase. It was a one-of-a-kind vase shipped in from Italy. She would have guests over for dinner and they would all talk for hours about how beautiful that vase was. But boys will be boys. My brother and I were wrestling one day after school and I knocked the vase over. It shattered into what seemed like a million pieces. We tried to fix it but nothing could be done. It was destroyed. My mom came home and she was highly upset. But I confessed and told her exactly what happened. She was mad because the vase was gone, but she forgave me because I decided to tell her the truth. Tell us the truth Minus."

The white detective reached into a folder and pulled out several pictures and placed them on the table. The first picture was that of a little girl in what seemed like a school picture. She had two ponytails in her hair, a blue dress on and was smiling from ear-to-ear. A brown globe and bookcase were behind her. He uncovered the first picture and showed the same girl on the ground with blood on her mouth and her shirt torn by a bullet that entered her chest. I put my head down and my eyes began to water.

The white detective pulled out a sheet of paper and handed me a pen. He said everything would be forgiven if I signed a confession. I grabbed the pen and began to do what I thought was right. Nothing could have changed what happened, but someone had to be held responsible for what that little girl went through. I wrote my first name on the paper and stopped when the door opened. Detective Murray stood in the doorway. The two detectives looked at each other and locked in eye contact. Detective Murray looked down at me and said, "What are you doing Minus?" He then looked at the other two detectives and asked harshly, "No. What are you two doing? You two know that you can't have this kid sign a confession without his lawyer being present. And he's still a minor, so a parent or guardian should be present also. Minus put that pen down and don't write another word. I suggest that you two call his guardian, or take him back to his cell."

Detective Murray snatched the paper and pen from the table and exited the room. Both of the detectives departed without speaking. Another officer came in and walked me back to the cell.

A lawyer named Mathew Mansfield was assigned by the state to serve as my public defender. He was a white guy in his mid-40s who seemed to have a relationship with the bottle. His eyes were droopy and swollen and he had an uneven five o'clock shadow on his face. He suggested that I plead guilty because the District Attorney would probably offer me 10 years for manslaughter. If I decided to go through a jury trial, I would face 10 to 20 years if found guilty. I didn't want to think about spending another week behind those bars, so I couldn't imagine being in that environment for 20 more years.

On the third day, my mom caught the bus to the Cook County Jail. A correctional officer escorted me to the visiting area where she sat in a chair wearing the blue scrubs she usually wore while working at Mercy Hospital. I was wearing an orange prison uniform, and silver handcuffs held my wrists together in front of me. She tilted her head towards the ceiling and grabbed the small gold plated cross that hung from her gold necklace. The officer unlocked my handcuffs and I sat down in front of the Plexiglas window. We both picked up the phone to hear each other's voice through the barrier that separated us.

"Now you know that you don't have no business in here Minus. Have you been reading your Bible?" my mom asked.

"Yeah, I've read it."

"You're looking terrible. Your eyes are all red and bags are under them. They're not bothering you in there are they?"

"No more than they're bothering anybody else in here."

"What are you going to do?"

"I don't know. The lawyer is saying that I should just plead guilty and take the years."

"Well I need to talk with him before you do anything. When do you go before the judge?"

"In a day or so."

"So do you really think you can handle the years?"

"I might not have a choice."

My mother put the phone down on the counter and stared at me. Her hurt-filled eyes tore through me. I attempted to look away, but I could not escape the guilt. I was her only child and she saw me traveling down a road without a future. This wasn't what she expected of me. She didn't like what I was becoming. Years could pass and our only contact would be through a dirty Plexiglas window. She picked up the phone and told me that she loved me, and left to go to work. I told her that I loved her and hung up the phone. She tried her best to keep me inside and away from the streets. But her protective arms weren't enough to keep me out of the system.

A few hours after my mother caught the bus to go to work, Hassan arrived at the jail and I met him in the visiting room. He was dressed casually in jeans and a black jacket that had the logo of Lil D's Barbershop on the upper right-hand corner. He sat down and noticed how weary my eyes were.

"You don't look too rested my friend. I'm guessing sleep hasn't been easy?" Hassan asked.

"I haven't really closed my eyes in a few weeks to tell you the truth."

"I understand. But I have some news that should take some of that pressure off. I talked to Ramon last night and we had a long conversation."

"Really?"

"We talked and he agreed to take himself out of it. So while you're in, you don't have to worry. About his people at least."

"I guess that's one less problem. What's going on out there?"

"There's motion. News cameras have been all around the projects to cover what happened to Blue and Sharonda. Some of Sharonda's family members and classmates held a candlelight vigil in memory of her the other day. I'm also working with a few religious groups to organize gun buy-back programs in Robert Taylor and Dearborn. People on the outside are paying attention to the projects today, but it took a lot for them to even recognize what we all see every day. But enough about that, what are they saying about the charge."

"They talking 10 to 20."

"Um. That's steep. I'll see what I can do out here. Until then, you have to keep your eyes and ears open while you're in. The only way to survive is to keep your mind active. So whenever you get a chance, read and exercise."

I put my right fist to the Plexiglas and he did the same. Hassan left the visiting room and I was led in handcuffs back to the holding cell.

The following morning, I was taken out of the cell at 7:30 a.m. by one of the correctional officers. He walked me into a room where I was then handcuffed to another inmate. We were escorted along with 15 other inmates to the Criminal Courts Building.

With our arms and legs shackled, we all walked slowly down the hall into the inmates' entrance of the courtroom. We were allowed time to confer with our lawyers before our charges were read by the judge. For the inmates who didn't have lawyers, the court offered to appoint one. As I looked around at the inmates in the courtroom, I noticed that all of us were black except for two older Hispanic males. It seemed as if the only people who were committing crimes in Chicago were black or Hispanic, or at least we were the only ones who were getting caught.

We all sat down and waited as the judge read each inmate's charge and asked for a plea. I decided that I would plead guilty so that I would have the chance to only be sentenced to 10 years. I knew that my life would never be the same, but I figured that starting over at the age of 25 was much better than starting over at 35. While waiting for my case to be called, I turned around and I saw my mom seated in the back of the courtroom next to Hassan. I nodded at them both and turned back around in the direction of the judge.

The judge was an older white woman who reminded me of Nancy Reagan. She had a mean nanny look and often squinted her eyes while staring angrily at the inmates who stood before her. Her thick glasses were perched on the bridge of her nose, and she would curl her lips in disgust when she read each charge. I walked to the defendant's podium and listened as she read my charges. While she was reading, Detective Murray walked into the courtroom and whispered into my lawyer's left ear. My lawyer whispered in my ear and I looked back up at the judge once she finished reading the charges. She asked me if I wanted to make a plea. I looked back at Detective Murray and I confidently said, "Not guilty." My lawyer then asked if I could be released on bail to the custody of my mom until the trial. He pointed out the fact that I was a musician and a member of the honor roll until middle school. The judge listened and then gave her remarks.

"I don't have a doubt in my mind that this young man

could've been or could be special. But what I have to look at is what he's charged with. He's charged with being involved in the murder of a little girl. Being that murder is the worst thing that a person can be charged with, it's even more disturbing when the victim is one of the most helpless members of our society; a child. And because of that, I will not grant the defendant a bond. The defendant must remain in the state's custody until a trial date is set."

The judge grabbed her gavel and hit the table. I nodded while looking back at my mom and Hassan. They both acknowledged me and I was escorted away from the courtroom in handcuffs.

My thoughts became my worst enemies once I returned to the jail cell. Staring at the same walls for hours forced me to wrestle with my anger and confusion. The sounds from the other inmates became muffled, and the only voice I could hear was the one that bounced around in my mind. I hated that voice. It was the only voice that knew the truth. It was a voice I could not silence no matter how hard I tried. Sometimes I could lie to the world, but I could never lie to that voice knowing that the voice would never lie to me.

The voice kept telling me I was at fault for what happened to Blue. I couldn't erase the images of Blue on the ground with his white sweatshirt soaked in blood. I let the words of Ramon scare me to the point that I was willing to kill my best friend. Fear drove me to the brink. I no longer knew myself. I feared that I would be unable to escape what I had become.

The Bullpen Therapy continued for three weeks. I began to think about the small things I took for granted while in the real world. Like sleeping in my own bed; eating a home cooked meal; waking up in the middle of the night to make a sandwich; being able to walk down the street to the corner store to buy chips or a soda; going out to see the latest movies; playing my grandfather's horn; and most importantly, hugging my mom.

I called my mom every day, but she did not return to the jail after the day of my court hearing. During a collect call, she said that the glass barrier, the orange jumpsuit and my shackled wrists gave her a migraine that Tylenol could not get rid of. So for her well being, I asked her to stay away from the jail.

After my court hearing, Detective Murray was the only familiar face that I saw in jail. He pulled me out of the cell one afternoon and took me into an interrogation room. On the table were three slices of pepperoni pizza that he bought from Phil's Pizza and a Styrofoam cup full of orange soda. Without hesitation, I tore into the pizza which tasted as good as a steak on that day.

"So, how are you keeping up in here Minus?" Detective Murray asked as I stuffed my mouth.

"I don't know how anyone can keep up in here."

"Yeah, we both know this isn't paradise. But I have some news for you. The day I told your lawyer to advise you to plead not guilty, we made an interesting discovery the night before. There were shells from two .38 handguns found at the murder scene, but we had no guns. Blue's gun was later discovered and I took it to a forensics specialist and had a ballistics test run on it. And what we found is that the bullets that killed Sharonda Lanvale didn't come from Blue's gun. I'm going to present this to the District Attorney tomorrow. He owes me one so he should at least look at this new evidence. If he does, I'll work on getting you released on bail."

I remained calm after hearing Detective Murray's news. By no means did I want to spend another minute in that place, but I also didn't want to set myself up for disappointment. If I had to spend time in jail, I wanted my mind to adapt to being in there. I didn't want to think about getting out until I knew that my name was going to be called. I had no control in the matter. So to remain focused on what I was up against, I accepted the present and tried hard not to fight my reality.

Eight days passed in March and I was moved to seven different cells in that month alone. By the time I was moved to the seventh cell, my legs were flimsy and my eyes were throbbing. The cell was moving sideways slowly and it only stopped when I closed my eyes. With all of the benches and cots occupied in the crowded cell, I sat down on the floor. I decided to keep my eyes closed. And for the first time since I had been arrested, I drifted into a deep sleep.

"Yeah, I think that's him. He was the punk sucker who was at the park that day!"

I opened my eyes and four inmates were standing over me. One of them grabbed my shirt and pulled me up. He then backed me into the wall and pressed his forearm against my chest as the other three surrounded me.

"I remember seeing you at the park. You took Nate's shoes and you're the reason why Lil Ronda's dead."

"I don't know what you talking about, Joe! I'm in here on other stuff."

"This fool is lying. Beat him down!"

With a closed fist, I swung at the dude who pressed his forearm against my chest. He released the grip that he had on my shirt and backed up. It was the only punch that I was able to land. I was hit in the stomach and slammed to the ground. I covered up as they all threw punches and stomped on me.

Two correctional officers rushed into the cell and the butt-kicking continued. One of the correctional officers swung his club without mercy to break up the fight. He hit some of the dudes who jumped me, but he also struck me in my back twice. Four more officers ran into the cell and one sprayed pepper spray. My eyes began to sting and my vision was blurred. My wrists were tied behind my back with plastic wires. The wires were so tight that my hands became numb. Two officers held me down. A third officer grabbed my ankles and tied them together. I was dragged by two officers out of the cell and placed into a closet-sized room. They took the plastic wires off of my wrists and ankles. One of the officers slammed the door shut and locked it. I could only hear the fast thumping of my heart and the sound of my own heavy breathing.

"Hall. Minus Hall! Get up!" A pudgy correctional officer yelled the following morning. I opened my eyes and wiped the cold out. I used my shirt to blow snot from my nose and spit phlegm into the toilet. As I stood up, I felt a sharp pain on the lower right side of my back. I limped to the correctional officer. "Come on Hall. Follow me." The officer placed handcuffs on my wrists and closed the door to the cell.

"Another day, another cell," I said as I staggered through the hall with the officer following a couple of steps behind me.

"Don't talk trash. I can get those boys who whipped your butt yesterday to come back for round two. I know you don't want that. I bet you the type who thinks he knows everything, but really don't know nothing. These cells are full of bastards like you," the officer said. "You should be feeling lucky, they called your name today. But we'll keep a spot for you in here. I'll give you until the summer when it's hot and sticky in this thing and suckers are sleeping all on top of each other. Yeah, that's when you'll be back. No matter how many chances y'all get, y'all find ways to return like this place is home."

The officer escorted me to the discharge area and I was processed out and released from the Cook County Jail. I exited from the jail with my coat under my right arm. To block the beaming sun from my eyes, I held my left hand a few inches above my forehead. With snow no longer on the ground, the brisk wind was the only reminder of winter. I inhaled deeply and cherished the fact that I was able to walk outside without being supervised or with chains around my wrists.

Hassan and my mom greeted me at the visitor's parking lot of the jail. I hugged my mother and a tear rolled down the side of her left cheek. I wanted to apologize, but I could not think of any words that would erase what she endured. She held me tight and said, "You're better than this." As we embraced, I felt the strength of a woman who never gave up on me. I could only show my appreciation by maturing and finding a way to become the man that she needed me to be.

Hassan approached me as my mom and I finished talking. I shook his hand and thanked him. He opened the passenger side door for my mom and I got into the back of his Volvo. Hassan started his car and drove south from the jail. He asked me if there was any place that I wanted to go before he took my mother and I home. I looked at Hassan and asked him if I could visit Blue's grave. While in jail, I was not prepared to face the fact that Blue was no longer here. It was an added burden that I tried hard not to think about. But my release forced me to deal with the truth. Blue was dead and it was time for me to pay my respects.

"You want to visit Blue at his grave?" Hassan asked as he looked at me through the rearview mirror and then glanced over to my mom. "Yeah, I think I'm ready to say goodbye," I said. My mom inhaled deeply and blew out hard. Hassan stopped the car and turned towards me. "Minus, I'm going to take you somewhere," Hassan said. "There's something you need to see."

CHAPTER 15

The only way to change is to kill old habits. - Clarence Hall

Hassan made a U-turn and drove east until we reached Michael Reese Hospital. I never enjoyed visiting the hospital. When I was younger, my mother took me to the clinic to get immunization shots so that I could register for elementary school. A nauseating feeling came over me as soon as I walked into the doctor's office. The depressed and sad looks on the faces of the patients caused me to feel uneasy. But as I got older, I realized that hospitals were a place that kept the rich alive, and the poor and uninsured away.

My mother remained in the lobby as Hassan and I caught the elevator to the ninth floor. Drops of sweat rolled down the side of my face and my stomach began to bubble. With each step, my legs felt as if they would buckle and send me crashing to the dusty hospital floor. We approached the room and Hassan knocked twice. He opened the door to a sight that I was glad to see, but unprepared to watch.

I peaked inside of the door and saw Blue lying on the bed. He wore a white hospital gown and several clear tubes were attached to his body. A large white bandage was stuck on the side of his neck and his left arm was in a sling. His eyes were closed and the heart monitor that stood next to his bed beeped every second. The beeps sped up. Blue turned and opened his right eye. He let out a soft yawn and drifted between closing and opening his eyes as he spoke.

"What's up my boy?" Blue asked. I paused for a couple of seconds before I responded.

"Nothing too much. Just glad to see you brah."

"Yeah, I'm here. Where else I'm gonna be? Joe, we can head down to the courts after I finish taking my nap. You ready to go? Let me get about five more minutes and I'm gonna grab my 23s and..."

In mid sentence, Blue stopped talking, closed his eyes and lapsed into a deep sleep. A nurse entered the room and asked if we could return on a day when Blue wasn't so heavily medicated. Hassan left the room. I walked towards the door and noticed Blue's notebook sitting on the counter to the right of the bed. The notebook was crumbled and dry specs of blood were splattered on the cover and across the first couple of pages. I turned to the last page where words were written in black ink and saw the date 2-20-89 scribbled at the top. I read the untitled poem.

We not of this world, this world is not r place/ We live n-side this land but this land dont feel r hate/ They fill r lives with hate and place us n this space, erased and then replaced while runnin a winless race/ Dont know what I chase, but I chase at a hard pace, and I chase until I realize that this chase is just a chase/ A chase without capture, a chase with no prey. Chasin to the point of chasin that whatever I'm chasin has gone away/ But I still chase until my feet can no longer defeat my fate, because faith wont save me from tha hell that is inches from my face.

I closed the notebook and placed it back on the counter. For several minutes, I stood still and watched as my closest friend attempted to recover from the bullets that hit him. At the same time, I wondered if we could find a way to recover from the pain that had overtaken us since the day it all started.

Blue was released from the hospital two weeks after my visit. He was shot four times and underwent several surgeries to remove the bullets. He was lucky to be alive and not paralyzed considering that one bullet grazed his neck. During his stay in the hospital, he was sedated on medications to allieviate the pain. I later found out that the medications were part of the reason that we were cleared from being responsible for what happened to Sharonda Lanvale.

Two weeks after my release from jail, I got an unexpected visit from Larry. He put me up on the latest happenings at Dunbar High and told me about some of the rumors that were floating around about the shooting. During our conversation, Larry also explained how the charges were dropped against Blue and I.

"For a while I thought that was it for you and Blue," Larry said as he sat on a basketball in my room while we listened to Biz Markie.

"Yeah, things had gotten scary for a minute. I don't know what went down, but I feel lucky to be sitting in this room right now."

"Well my father visited Blue after he woke up from his coma. Blue was so drugged up from the medication that he told my father the entire story and other illegal stuff that he had done in the past."

"Blue snitched on himself? He really must have been high on those hospital meds."

"My father disregarded most of what Blue told him, but listened when he gave him the whereabouts of his gun. He said that Blue hid his gun in this vacant apartment in Dearborn. My father found it and sent it to a ballistics lab for a test."

"So that's what cleared us huh?"

"Not really. My father said that the D.A. wasn't going to drop the charges until the actual murder weapon was found. You guys got lucky when the cops arrested this guy near the Robert Taylor homes on a felony charge. He was so desperate to try to get his charges dropped that he told police who really shot the girl and where they could find the gun."

Two months after Larry's visit, a guy by the name of Rico was convicted of murdering Sharonda Lanvale. Rico was sitting under the shed with Fat Nate and Winky on the day of the shooting. Apparently, Rico was the person who shot at us. As he fired shots, Sharonda Lanavale ran across the street in the direct path of the gunfire. Rico, who was a part-time runner for Ramon Lanvale, turned himself in once the word got back to Ramon that he was the shooter. Rico was sentenced to 20 years in prison.

Fat Nate and Winky never retaliated. Through Hassan, I returned Fat Nate's shoes and I'm sure that Ramon played a part in making sure they squashed the situation as well.

I never lived on the South Side again. One week after my release, my mom and I moved back into my grandmother's home in Oak Park. Our old apartment had too many bad memories, so we both decided that moving would separate us from the problems that could have easily returned to those red steps. On the day we moved to my grandmother's house, my mother warned me against returning to my old neighborhood. She believed that I was no longer safe in that section of the city. The South Side had caused her too much pain and she made a vow to do all that she could to make sure we never went back.

While living at my grandmother's home, I spent most of my days playing the horn or listening to my grandfather's dusties. Stevie Wonder's album was spinning on the record player when my mom walked into the living room and handed me an envelope with New Trier High School's logo on the upper right-hand corner. The envelope was from the school's music department. Inside the envelope was a letter stating my acceptance into the music program.

The school was located in an area that seemed like it was a million miles away from the South Side, but the time had come for me to take a step in another direction. Even if I was being used to make the school appear to be a "fair" place that accepted all types, the opportunity was there and I needed to take advantage of it to do better for myself. My grandfather used to tell me, "The only way to change is to kill old habits." I needed to destroy the flaws in my behavior and start new. Changing schools was the first step.

My mother transferred me out of Dunbar and I enrolled at New Trier High during the second week of April. I woke up at five o'clock in the morning in order to catch the train and two buses to Winnetka. There were no metal detectors, security guards, or book bag checks at the entrance. Each classroom at New Trier contained a 24-inch TV/VCR, four personal computers, and a CD-ROM player. The covers of my textbooks were intact, the pages were crisp, and there were only a few names on the front pages. The fact that I was in an entirely different environment became more evident during lunch. I sat down with five other members of the jazz band in the cafeteria. My friends at Dunbar used the lunch period to talk about girls, basketball and the latest shoes. But the students at New Trier discussed their soccer games and geek movies like *Star Trek* and *Alien Nation*. A few of the students attempted to be hip by rapping aloud, dressing in urban gear, or using slang. They tried hard to capture the style and swagger of the South Side, but they were all pretenders.

In my first two months in the jazz band, I traveled to Milwaukee, Kansas City and Detroit. We performed in front of hundreds of people and I got the chance to meet some of the top jazz musicians and groups in America. New Trier gave me the opportunity to experience another side of life.

But as summer approached, I began to miss the South Side. I missed seeing the girls stroll through the halls of Dunbar like they were modeling at a fashion show. I missed hanging around Larry, Peanut and listening to Meathead's silly jokes. As long as the sun came up, we could count on Meathead saying something that would have the entire crew cracking up for hours. The life that I lived on the South Side seemed so distant. But the hardest part was starting over without Blue.

I spoke with Blue over the phone twice after he was released from the hospital. Both of the conversations were short and we never set aside time to play ball or hang out. Maybe it was a sign of us getting older. Or it could've been that we just didn't think the same anymore. Or the pain of what we went through was so severe that being around each other would only remind us of a time that we wished we could forget. But I couldn't forget what Blue and the entire South Side meant to me. Against my mother's warnings, I caught the train to my old neighborhood two weeks into the summer break. My hair was in need of a trim, so my first visit was to Lil D's Barber Shop.

Walking into Lil D's Barber Shop for the first time in almost six months was like returning home. The debates, the jokes, the boosters and unforgettable stories made the barbershop more than a place to get a haircut. It was a spot where young boys learned and old men voiced their thoughts on how they saw the world. My return gave the barbers more fodder for their on-going conversations.

"Hey, it's the trumpet boy!" "Horn boy, play something for a dollar." Two barbers shouted as I walked in.

"Whipper snapper, who said you could quit? I still have you on my payroll. I got some work for ya and I need you to bring that horn back. It brought some much needed ambiance to my classy establishment," Lil D said as the barbershop exploded in laughter.

"Sorry Lil D, I can't accept your job offer. I don't stay this way anymore," I replied.

"Aww, see what happens when you give these youngsters employment? They take your money and then they get too big for ya. It's like the more I give, the less I receive." Lil D got more laughs as I walked to Hassan's chair.

"Minus, long time no look young bro," Hassan said as I sat in his chair.

"I've been making it. You know how it goes."

"I heard you're up there with the 'burb' kids. How is it up north?"

"It's super slow up there in Winnetka. I had a lot more fun at Dunbar because all of my friends were there. I guess I needed a change though."

"True. Speaking of Dunbar, a girl who said she was a classmate of yours stopped by a few weeks ago. She asked if you still worked here. I think her name was Meka."

"Oh, yeah! I think you mean Meta. I'll give her a call."

"So have you spoken with Blue?"

"Naw. I talked to him a week after he got out of the hospital and I remember him telling me that you wanted him to move in with you."

"Yeah, I knew that he'd get stuck if he stayed in Dearborn, so I offered to let him stay at the apartment I share with my fiancé. That allowed him to get away from the grind for a minute. I got him to enroll at Dunbar and he entered this poetry contest. His poem was even published in a newsletter for students who attend school in the city. But after two months, he left my apartment and stopped going to school. I talked to a few people who told me that he went back to selling in Dearborn. I went over there to talk to him and he agreed to come back. But I haven't heard from him since."

"Man, I'll try to get in touch with him."

"If you do, tell him to give me a call."

Hassan finished cutting my hair and took off the white apron that was around my neck. "Be safe out here Minus. I know these are your people, but some people in the streets are hungrier than ever." Hassan extended his right fist and I did the same.

I shook hands with all of the barbers as I walked out. I then caught the bus to the Dearborn Homes. The projects had not changed much since the day that I was escorted out in handcuffs six months earlier. A few kids flipped on old mattresses and played in patches of dirt where grass used to be. Some mothers looked out of their apartment windows to keep an eye out for their kids as they played near the areas where the hypes and dealers did business.

I walked to the courtyard and approached the green bench where Blue usually sold. A boy who looked to be a few years younger than me sat on the bench and handed vials to the hypes who approached him. The boy looked at me and put his hand near his waist as I got closer to the bench.

"No need for that. Just wanna know something," I said. The boy removed his hand from under his shirt and remained quiet as he continued to look out for the hypes.

"I'm trying to find Blue. Just wanna know if he's around here."

"Who are you?" The boy asked in a raspy voice without making eye contact with me.

"I'm Minus."

"Minus! You went down with Blue back when the police shot him." the boy said, making direct eye contact for the first time since I had approached him.

"Yeah, that's me."

"Joe, you have been gone for a while. Blue don't come around that much."

"What you mean?"

"Blue was back out here for a minute, but he changed up when Tony got out. They say Tony hooked up with somebody when he was in Cook County who gave him some work. Tony got out and put a team together with Blue a few months back. They took a trip to Iowa and set up shop. He still comes out here every now and then to pick up and drop off work."

"Iowa, huh?"

"They weren't ready, Blue and them got those country boys on their toes."

Drug dealing was Blue's way of getting the most out of what the Dearborn environment offered. He dedicated himself from daybreak to midnight to an occupation that paid well, but had consequences of jail or death. There was something about the business that made him believe that there was light at the end. I could hardly see the light from my view, but Blue saw something that made him commit to being the best at what he was doing. In a sense, it did allow him to move away from Dearborn. But I'm not sure if he ever really made it out.

I turned away from the youngster on the bench and watched the hand-to-hand transactions in the courtyard and wondered about all who played a part in what I was seeing. I observed as the dealers and hypes sacrificed their lives to sell or buy a high. I thought about how it affected C-Roy. He didn't come off as a bad person, but his drug addiction changed what he could have been. Even if he would have returned to be with my mom and me, I doubt if he could have ever loved his family more than he did his habit.

I left the Dearborn courtyard and began walking to my old block. The vibe on my old block reminded me of the memorable summers of the past. A group of young boys shot basketball on a dark blue plastic crate that was nailed to a wooden light pole as the girls played patty cake on the sidewalk. The latest record from De La Soul was blasting from a parked blue and white 1985 Chevy Cutlass. A teenage girl smiled and placed her hands on her hips as she stood in front of a guy leaning on the driver's side door of the Cutlass. Directly across the street, a group of old men laughed and talked so loud their voices could be heard over the music that vibrated from the Cutlass. They gathered around a table where two of the men stared quietly at the chess pieces on a chessboard. I continued to walk through the neighborhood until I reached my old apartment. Meathead, Calvin and Peanut stood near the red steps.

"Can we call you Mr. Suburbia now?" Meathead yelled as I approached.

"Naw, you can almost call me daddy if your momma keeps acting right." I jibbed at Meathead as we all laughed.

"That's alright Minus. You see these new 23's that I have? All courtesy of Ms. Hall. She somehow finds a way to keep me looking better than you."

"I hear you Meat. But try to pull one of those Dunbar chicks before you step up to a woman who has a job."

"Man, I got so many girls up there that they fighting just to hold my lunch tray. I even got the finest girl at the school on me."

"Who, Imani Grier? You don't have what it takes to even eat at the same lunch table with her."

"Imani? She ain't the finest girl at Dunbar."

"Are you kidding me? Imani was in her own league the last time I saw her. And unless Vanity from *The Last Dragon* is at Dunbar, no girl is outshining Imani when it comes to looks."

"That's the thing. It's been a while since anyone has seen her."

"So she transferred schools to get away from lames like you, huh?"

"She wish. You know she was a mule for that boy who used to pick her up from school everyday."

"Wasn't his name Troy or something like that?"

"I'm not really down with dropping names. But I heard old boy sold up there in the Wild Hunneds. He was breaking her off like half a stack every time she went to pick up a few packages. He sent her to get a few bricks of cocaine from

Indiana back in April. They say right before she got back to the Chi, police pulled her over and found those bricks inside of a spare tire in her trunk. She been on lockdown ever since. So no, she ain't the finest girl at Dunbar."

"How am I supposed to believe you? You would tell a lie even if there was no such thing as one."

"Meathead ain't fibbing on this one Minus," Calvin jumped in. "Your girl is facing about a dime or more on lock."

"Do you all ever see that girl Meta who hung out with Imani?" I asked.

"Yeah, I see her around school. She tries to give it to me too. But I don't really mess with those redbones like that. I only deal with fine chocolate chicks. They got the best bodies and the best rhythm. Those redbones are just too stiff." Meathead said.

"I doubt if that girl even knows your name Meat. But I'll let you wrestle with that fantasy in your head. I'm going back to my grandmother's house so I'll see you boys later."

"Hey man, I bet you're gonna be looking like *Leave it to Beaver* the next time we see you."

"Meathead, the next time I see you, your mother is going to be bringing me breakfast in her bed. But on the real, give me a call the next time you all play ball at Larry's house. I'll come back down to teach you some lessons on the court."

I threw up a peace sign to Meathead, Calvin and Peanut and I headed to the corner store. Once inside, I purchased a bag of Hot Fries, seven 10-cent pieces of bubble gum, and a grape soda. The cashier placed my goods in a brown paper bag and I took the items outside. I sat down at the edge of the curb directly in front of the store and began munching on the Hot Fries. For nearly 20 minutes, I observed the people, the cars and listened to the sounds that resonated on the street that I once called home.

During the bus ride to my grandmother's house, two boys a few years younger than me got on at South Princeton Avenue. One of the boys wore a long white T-shirt, blue jean shorts and black Cortez Nikes. The other boy sported a dark blue Walter Payton jersey, black jeans and black, white and red number 4 edition of the 23s.

The boy with the white T-shirt laughed uncontrollably as he sat next to his friend who wore the Walter Payton jersey. The boy in the Walter Payton jersey breathed heavily and his jersey was stretched around the collar. He popped his knuckles and looked at a scratch that was located near his right elbow. He then placed his index finger on his tongue and wiped off his shoes."

"Damn Joe, you didn't have to beat Corey down like that man," the boy with the white T-shirt said as his friend remained quiet. "But I guess you did have a reason. I mean he stepped on your new 23s. I would have beat his ass down for that too!"

Twenty-three changed who we were. It gave us attitude, it measured our coolness, and it turned our desires into hate. We did the unthinkable to get our hands on 23 because we believed that ownership gave us control. But we could never control 23 because we were the ones who were captivated by that powerful number. It became larger than a basketball player and his shoes because we made it that way. We gave 23 its own world and we duped ourselves into never deviating from the rules. It was our rules that allowed them to give 23 style, create hysteria, and inflate the price. Our rules didn't allow us to walk in the wrong place with them, or others to accidentally walk on them. We are responsible for what 23 gives and what it eventually takes away.

One month after my visit to the South Side, my mom and I moved into a three bedroom apartment near Lincoln Park. We transported most of our furniture to the new apartment on a Saturday afternoon in August. That evening, my grandmother suggested that we spend one more night at her home. During our Saturday night gathering, my grandmother and mother prepared a dinner that would have rivaled any meal that was served on the last Thursday of November. My mom invited a few friends from her job and a couple of my grandmother's neighbors also joined us. They served baked chicken, macaroni and cheese, corn bread, string beans and dressing. For dessert, my grandmother baked a red velvet cake and a sweet potato pie. After dessert, we watched my mom's favorite movie, *Black Girl*. Shortly before midnight, the guests went home and we all decided to get some rest.

My eyes opened a few hours after lying down in the bed. I rolled back and forth while seeking a comfortable space. The covers were partially wrapped around me and my left leg hung off the side of the mattress. While turning over on my stomach, the pillow fell to the floor. I pulled back the covers and stood up.

The alarm clock read 5:42 a.m. I stumbled to the bathroom, gargled and wiped my face with a warm damp towel. Instead of returning to bed, I walked into my grandmother's pitch-black living room. While searching for the lamp, I bumped my right foot on the edge of the wooden end table and the telephone fell to the floor. I turned on the lamp and sat on the couch with the phone in my right hand. I took the receiver off of the hook and dialed Meta's number.

"Hello," Meta answered the phone with a rough and uneven whisper.

"I do believe in you," I said.

"What? Who is this?"

"According to you, I'm the boy who has eyes like a tiger."

"Eyes like a…oh, is this Minus?"

"It's kinda cool that you got it right on the first try."

"Maybe it's just luck or I'm still dreaming."

"Your eyes are probably still closed, but you're not dreaming."

"I wish I were. What time is it?"

"I'm hoping this is a good time to talk."

"Let me get some things straight. So, you leave your neighborhood, you leave the school, and I don't hear from you for months. I reach out to get in touch with you and I get no information about where you are and what you're doing. But you decide to call me on a random day, at a random time so that we can talk. Seriously Minus, I want to hang up. But I fear that if I hang up, I might not ever hear from you again."

"I was hoping that you wouldn't hear from me again because I would rather see you. I can stay on the phone right now and tell you everything that I need to say. But if I did, you wouldn't be able to get back to that dream you were having."

"Yeah, it would be nice if I could get back to my dream, but I also would like to know why you've been missing and what took you so long to call."

"What are you doing in about seven hours?"

"Hopefully, I'll be well rested so that I can start my day."

"Why don't you start your day with me?"

"What do you mean?"

"What I mean is that I want you to meet me at Ford City mall. We can catch a movie and eat a deep dish pizza. Then, we can sit down and I'll tell you why we haven't seen each other in so long."

"I guess that's OK. What time do you want to meet?"

"At two o'clock. You should have gotten enough Z's by then."

"Whatever Minus. You just be there at two. I'm about to go back to sleep now. I don't like to wake up before I can see the sun."

"I don't know whether I should say goodnight or good morning."

"Just say bye. But before I hang up, I'm happy that you finally gave me an answer. It's good to know that you believe in me too. I'll see you later, Minus."

I hung up with Meta and placed the phone back on the end table. On the side of the end table were two packed boxes that my mom and I were taking to our new apartment. I opened one of the boxes and began searching through it. Inside were pictures, old post cards, tapes, and the trumpet case. I grabbed the case and pulled out my grandfather's trumpet. With the trumpet in my right hand, I opened the front door and walked outside. The darkness of the early morning sky began to give itself to an emerging sun. I stood at the top of the porch, absorbed the stillness of dawn and listened. I placed the trumpet to my lips and began to play. The West Side of Chicago hadn't heard those sounds that early in years. I figured the neighborhood needed a morning wake up call.

TWENTY-THRΣƎ

A NOVEL